"For ~~c~~
so stu

"Stubborn? Perhaps that's because you always want things your way," Laura answered.

Chase pulled on his earlobe, a sure sign that he was getting irritated. Good, she thought, because his cologne was driving her crazy. The familiar scent made Laura remember how it had been between the two of them. And now she couldn't stop thinking about how it had been to kiss him.

Maybe that's why she turned her head. She later told herself she had turned to let him know just whom he was dealing with eye to eye.

"We're not buddies, Chase. Don't think that this is beginning for us. There's no happy-ever-after, no riding off into the sunset and no romantic reunion here," Laura said.

She wanted to say more. She'd had more to say about her hurt and disappointment, but then she made the mistake of looking at his lips....

Books by Michelle Monkou

Kimani Romance

Sweet Surrender

Kimani Press Arabesque

Open Your Heart
Finders Keepers
Give Love
Making Promises
Island Rendezvous

MICHELLE MONKOU

became a world traveler at three when she left her birthplace of London, England, and moved to Guyana, South America. She then moved to the United States as a young teen. An avid reader, her diverse cultural experiences set the tone for her vivid imagination. It wasn't long before the stories in her head became stories on paper.

In the middle of writing romances, she added a master's in international business to her bachelor in English. Michelle was nominated for the 2003 Emma Award for Favorite New Author. She continues to write romances with complex characters and intricate plots. Visit her Web site for further information and to sign up for her newsletter and contest at www.michellemonkou.com. Write to her at P.O. Box 2904, Laurel, Maryland 20709, or e-mail her at michellemonkou@comcast.net.

HERE *and* NOW

Michelle Monkou

KIMANI ROMANCE

Acknowledgment:

Family hugs to Doreen Monkou, Navlette Gordon, Angela Gordon, Donsha Monkou, Kristina Monkou, Morgan Monkou, Gabrielle Samuels, and Amber Monkou—Girl Power!

A big "Thank You" to Stephanie Sabol, MPT, at Maximum Performance Physical Therapy for sharing insight on the profession, scenarios for injured athletes, and treatment. Any errors or omissions are mine.

KIMANI PRESS™

RECYCLED PAPER

ISBN-13: 978-0-373-86002-9
ISBN-10:   0-373-86002-1

HERE AND NOW

Copyright © 2007 by Michelle Monkou

www.kimanipress.com

Printed in U.S.A.

Dear Reader,

Welcome to the Masterson family, four close-knit siblings that made it through life's ups and downs without their parents. Each family member has a story to tell. We met the eldest brother, Pierce Masterson, in my first Kimani Romance title, *Sweet Surrender*. But it wouldn't be fair to have love visit only one sibling.

In this title, *Here and Now*, the Masterson family saga continues with a perfectly matched couple— Laura Masterson and Chase Dillard. Who better to appreciate the sexy physique of a sprinter than the beautiful physical therapist that was his first love.

And when you've turned the last page of Laura and Chase's story, you'll be happy to know that you haven't seen the last of Laura; she'll perform a lifesaving technique in the next episode of the Masterson family series. So stay tuned for the youngest sibling Omar's story. Omar is a stone-cold player who meets his match in a rising hip-hop star and budding actress, Stacy Watts. Theirs will be a young love full of romance, with a touch of spice.

Please check out my Web site—www.michellemonkou.com— for contests, registering on my mail list and posting on my blog, Dream Like a Star. If you prefer snail mail, write to P.O. Box 2904, Laurel, MD 20709, or e-mail me at michellemonkou@comcast.net.

Chapter 1

Chase Westfield pulled out his personal data assistant and reviewed the list of reminders. Technically he didn't need the mental nudge. Every year, since high school, he remembered one particular birthday. First love, like a meteor, had the power to crash into the system with enough impact to throw every feeling, thought or memory off kilter. One woman had such a forceful effect on his system.

He sighed heavily, fingering the thin red ribbon tied around the small gift box. The box fit neatly on his palm. But its meaning was larger than anything in his office. His birthday gift served dual purposes, one more important than the other, that included being considered a peace offering.

"Mr. Westfield, the staff meeting is about to begin," his secretary prompted.

"Thanks, Sandy."

She didn't move until he looked up from the gift box and set it aside. Chase still had to get used to the various meetings that consumed his entire day. Every appointment appeared to come with a special announcement tag or a bold heading marked as important or urgent. All these command performances grated on his nerves. He was a man used to listening to his own internal directives.

Now, a typical day was spent in meetings with the department, the track team and assistant coaches. If he could manage, he escaped to the track field armed with a stop watch. While his peers headed for home around five o'clock, he ended his day with more coaching and the occasional one-on-one mentoring sessions.

With no background in coaching, he had to rely on his college coach's tricks and tips to nudge the best from his team. By year-end, heck by month-end, these young men had to understand that talent alone didn't breed success. Razor sharp focus, coupled with one hundred and ten percent commitment, had to become their mantra.

After all, he should know. The emotional high from winning a medal didn't do anything for those days when consistently crossing the finish line in second or third place threatened rankings in the sport.

He opened his desk drawer to return the small box. His hand paused over the gift. Finding a way to present this token, especially on her first day of work, might prove to be difficult. Well, presenting it was one thing, having it accepted could be near impossible since he'd broken almost every promise that he'd made. He frowned, now wrapped up in his worry.

Shaking off the doubts that tested his conscience, he headed for the conference room. His tardiness already earned him a reputation that made him the butt of many jokes. He'd better hurry. Meanwhile, the clock in the hallway gave him three minutes before the meeting started. As he approached the coffee machine, the steaming pot begged for his attention.

"What the heck," he muttered, heading toward the scent of freshly brewed, addictive coffee.

Training as a sprinter didn't afford him the luxury to deviate from a strict diet. To his credit, he carried a super lean physique with a metabolism likened to the Japanese bullet train. Now as head coach, retired from his first profession at the age of twenty-six with a blown Achilles tendon on one heel and a torn ACL in the other knee, he enjoyed breaking the rules that were once his personal code.

Some people who suffered self-medicated with booze. He chose to drown his sorrows in vast quantities of coffee.

He sipped the dark liquid, savoring the robust flavor. Now his day could begin. With a ready smile, he pushed open the conference room door. A quick survey showed most, if not all, of the staff in attendance. The clock on the conference room wall now declared him five minutes late. Darn!

"Ah, Chase has joined us. Okay, let's begin."

Chase peered at Roger Freeman, his boss, trying to read if sarcasm was in play. Freeman's wide grin set his mind at ease. However, muffled laugher and teasing about his tardiness from the rear of the room followed him to his seat.

Freeman held up his hand until there was some semblance of calm. "As you know, we had a little shake-up in staff personnel three weeks ago. Out of the slight chaos we managed to land our very own Olympic medalist, Chase Westfield." Freeman paused, allowing his staff's roar of approval to play out. "Before we begin the staff meeting, I'd also like to introduce our latest addition. I'm pleased with our recruitment efforts in adding another qualified physical therapist to our staff. We can count our lucky stars that the board of regents didn't recommend any cost cutting measures for our departments." Freeman stepped out of the room.

A dull murmur filled the room. Much to Chase's embarrassment Freeman had mentioned his arrival to the department as if it were something new. Of course, he knew what an asset he was to any university, even if in name only. At least his colleagues played along with their excited boss at each meeting.

However, at each meeting, mentioning Freeman didn't eclipse their unease when cutbacks and the board of regents were also part of the discussion. Topics like this placed Chase at a disadvantage. Chase's income had spiked like a rocket as he won numerous championships, broke records and raked in various endorsement deals. Today, he commiserated with a few of his fellow coworkers out of a need to belong, to fit in with his new world.

He'd turned into an everyday kind of man now.

Freeman stepped back into the room. He was always the character, with his disheveled, shocking white hair and twinkling, vivid blue eyes, now grinning with boyish exuberance. He turned toward them. "She's here."

His pose reminded Chase of a game show host opening the magical Door No. 1 with a great deal of theatrics. He'd heard that his boss belonged to an amateur actors group.

Chase eased to the edge of his seat, craning his neck to see around the head of another eager observer. As an afterthought, he set down his empty coffee cup on a nearby window sill. He didn't trust his hands with the task of holding on to anything. Anticipation zipped through his body as if on roller blades, shooting to the tips of his fingers and toes. Jitters from the stomach-knotting tension grew without regard to his fervent wish to remain calm. His nervousness took him back to his competitive days, waiting in the starter box for the race to begin.

And then, Laura Masterson entered the room.

A few of the men sitting nearby paused in their conversations.

Chase gulped.

The girl he knew on the cusp of womanhood had rounded the turn. Nothing less than a confident, sexy young woman stood at the front of the room.

He'd have loved to offer up a whistle of appreciation. But she didn't deserve anything so common. All he could settle for was his heart beating on hyper-speed on the verge of a panic attack.

"Welcome. Welcome. Come on in. They don't bite," Freeman offered with a deep, underlying chuckle. He indicated an empty chair close to him. "Everyone, please introduce yourself to Laura Masterson, our new physical therapist." Freeman's chest puffed with pride like an old lion looking over his dominion.

One by one, the staff welcomed Laura. She acknowledged with a soft, personal smile for each person. What they said to her held no importance for him. Right now, memory had to catch up with the current, real version of his former love.

Only the woman in the front of the room mattered, sporting a tightly secured ponytail, a stylish navy blue pantsuit on her slender frame and sensible shoes.

Chase eased back in his chair, pushing it back toward the wall. He wasn't hiding, but simply wanted to lengthen the time that he could study her without her knowledge. He'd broken her heart once. He didn't expect her initial reaction to be along the lines of a happy family reunion.

As his colleagues stated their names, Chase scrutinized Laura's face noting that she wore more makeup now. The soft colors accenting her eyes enhanced their roundness. Years ago, he used to trail the length of her nose playing connect the dots with the tiny freckles sprinkled against the natural beige tone along the bridge. The small rounded tip of her nose had a cute uplift that got her teased as a teen for being a snobby nose. And who would have figured that when provoked, her dainty small mouth could curse like a sailor?

Right now, that small mouth with full lips shimmered with a coppery glaze. She smiled at each introduction. He noticed that her lips trembled ever so slightly. Occasionally, she ran a shaky hand over her hair, adding credence to his summation. Wow, she was nervous.

With only two colleagues separating her from him, Chase hoped that she wouldn't be too blown away by his sudden appearance. He took a deep breath. His hands grew clammy. Heck, he couldn't deny that he also was nervous.

Then Laura shifted her ready smile from the assistant coach to him. Her eyes widened and the smile drooped as her mouth shut in a decisive snap. With an imperceptible shake of the head, she again turned on the smile, reviving it to its original brilliance. Gone, however, was the warm, curiosity in her face. He knew a fake smile when he saw one and he could sense a deep-seated grudge with his eyes closed.

"Miss Masterson, I'm Chase Westfield."

"He's the senior assistant director of athletics and head coach for the men's track team," Freeman added, still beaming from his chair.

"Very nice to meet you. I know that you'll like it here. Welcome." His voice had lost its smooth quality and turned into a froggy version.

Just as well. If he had any more time to talk, he may have slipped and turned it personal. He could've commented on how the longer hair suited her with the thick ponytail lying over one shoulder. Or follow that compliment by mentioning how well the navy blue suit fitted her slender body. And the curves had become curvier. But that would get him punched in the eye.

As a sophomore in high school, he'd patted her behind as part of a bet. The act had earned him a solid punch to his right eye and ridicule from his friends. Like that day, he didn't walk away from a challenge. Did he really expect that Laura would run carefree into his arms with sincere well wishes?

No, not when he'd broken her heart.

"Laura, Chase temporarily oversees your department. The reporting structure is in a state of flux." Freeman's voice boomed over the conversation buzz.

Laura sucked in her breath. She'd often wondered if constantly thinking about someone could make them appear. Being level-headed proved to be difficult in this case. She felt as if she'd done an aerobics tape on fast forward. All she could see was the instant that she moved from the assistant coach, whatever-his-name was, to Chase. That image looped repeatedly. Then his lips moved. She tried to concentrate on what he said. But, her thoughts bounced around like a ping-pong ball with one possibility, then another and even a third idea of why she was standing in front of Chase. When his lips stopped moving, she knew it was her cue to speak and hopefully sound sensible.

"Thank you," she responded. Of course, "kiss my butt" would've been more appropriate. She'd save that for later.

"Laura, you can take a seat. Then, we'll get started." The boss pointed her toward a vacant chair.

Grateful that it wasn't near Chase, she hurried over to the opposite side of the room. Although on the other side of the room, the distance didn't help matters when she had such a clear view of his profile. The 90's haircut had been replaced by a layered cut along the sides and back. She remembered how soft his hair felt when she'd ran her fingers along the wavy grain of his hair.

And that thick head of hair always belonged to a handsome face. Chase's smooth skin earned her envy with its clear, unblemished, even tone. Why were long lashes, a milk chocolate complexion and chiseled features wasted on someone like him? She wanted to work the paper from her pad into a ball and throw it at his profile. If she thought that Mr. Freeman wouldn't be appalled and fire her on the spot, she'd let one rip.

When he stood at the end of the meeting, she couldn't take her eyes off him. And why didn't he look the least bit surprised or uncomfortable at seeing her? Right now, he chatted with his colleagues, slapping their backs in friendly fashion, gesticulating with grand hand motions. He was all business. His coolness irritated her.

In a quick moment, he looked up, caught her eye and then looked away. Good, she hadn't blinked or averted her gaze. Although his eyes didn't rest on her for any lengthy period, it was enough that their eyes connected. She kept up her scrutiny. Seconds later, she was rewarded when she noticed him tugging at his collar. The dashing smile had faded. Maybe the act had come to an end.

"Laura and Chase, stop in my office for a few minutes," Freeman invited.

"After you." Chase stepped over to the side, exaggerating the distance provided to her.

Laura walked past, careful to maintain the distance between them.

"Have a seat." Freeman indicated the chairs in front of his desk.

Laura sat and glanced over at the chair next to her to see if Chase intended to step away from the door to join them. She looked up at Freeman to see if he'd tolerate Chase not exactly following directions.

"I'll stand, thank you," Chase offered, folding his arms and leaning against the door frame.

"Suit yourself." Freeman turned his attention to Laura. "When you'd interviewed a month ago, Coach Nichols was still employed."

Laura nodded and leaned forward. Chase had not been mentioned when she underwent the extensive interview process.

"Coach Nichols suffered a family crisis that required his immediate attention even though the school year had begun. We got wind that Chase was being heavily recruited after he retired. How

lucky were we? Still can't believe that he's here."
Freeman's open admiration matched its owner's
effusive nature.

If Laura didn't have an ounce of admiration for
Chase, Freeman could brainwash her in minutes
with his enthusiasm.

"Let's not overwhelm Miss Masterson. I'll be
chatting with her after your meeting. Hopefully,
she'll want to work with me, the poor substitute
to the renowned Coach Nichols," Chase remarked
in a droll voice.

Freeman chuckled, his wide girth vibrating with
his amusement. He pushed back his chair and
stood. Laura looked into his eyes which reminded
her of Newman's intense blue ones. She really
enjoyed being in Freeman's company. His easy-
going attitude set her at ease. She wished that he
had more to say or that she could create a reason
to delay heading off with the man standing behind
her.

"Let me get going to my next meeting," Freeman said. "I've got a busy morning ahead of me.
Laura, again, we are so pleased that you're on
board. Chase, take care of this young lady, she's
valuable to our department and your team." Laura

headed for the door where Chase still leaned, looking like he didn't have a care.

He grinned at her.

She didn't return the gesture.

He had the audacity to wink at her. They walked down the hall with him leading the way. Freeman walked with her, also heading to his next appointment. They approached a cross section of hallways. To her dismay, Freeman waved and headed down another hall. She stopped, debating whether to follow Freeman, in which case, she'd have to think of a reasonable excuse to be tagging behind him.

"Laura, aren't you coming? My office is this way."

Again he grinned. With a long sigh at Freeman's retreating figure, she reminded herself that she was a big girl. She could handle her ex-boyfriend popping unexpectedly into her life. Offering a tight smile, she followed him. But he slowed his steps, until they were shoulder to shoulder.

"How's the family? Is everyone still in Hampton Mews?" Chase asked.

"Fine. For now, everyone is in Maryland." Good gracious, now he wanted to have small talk.

"Your brother? Pierce?"

"Married." Now where did that smugness in her tone come from? They'd only discussed marriage once. It had been in the final words before they went their separate ways. Four years later, she had done a good job pushing her feelings six feet under and sealing them with a thick layer of indifference. The effort took hard work, discipline and focus. The three reasons he'd used for calling it quits.

Chase pushed open a set of double doors with a bright EXIT sign overhead. She stepped through, then stopped short. Laura looked up at him for an explanation.

"Figured we could delay the trip to my office for a few minutes," Chase explained.

She nodded, still not sure why they were outside the building. Outdoors, she could regroup. Laura raised her face, enjoying the sting of the brisk coolness even in Georgia. Autumn with its crisp temperatures, golden leaves and themes of harvest appealed to her sense of family. Her mother had said that it was a time for gathering those close to you. As the long winter came, you use the longer time indoors to bond. But with four children and no father, maybe that story was to keep them from fighting and arguing.

"Never could understand why you loved the cold weather so much." Chase looked at her, bearing a wide smile. Without lingering, he continued leading the way from the building across the road to the enclosed stadium.

Traffic on campus during the midmorning hours didn't differ too much from morning rush hour. Mostly compact cars zipped past, screeching to a halt at the four-way stop signs that dotted the campus roads, then racing off with tires squealing. Students on bikes made up the other major group, while clusters of young men and women hurried along the sidewalks and footpaths.

Campus life energized Laura with its similarity to a small city. There was lots to do and see. As a student, she'd thought of pursuing a teaching career, maybe even becoming a professor. These dreams she'd shared with Chase. Out in the real world, she hadn't had time to think about what she really wanted to do. Maybe seeing her big brother, Pierce, settle down with his family made her realize that she was letting time slip away.

Chase recited facts about the University of

Atlanta, dates of key political figures who had been students and the institution's rankings in various athletic divisions.

In other words, her feet rested on hallowed grounds. In her small way, she hoped to participate in making an athlete's dream come through. She'd tried to do the same with Chase in much different circumstances and with negative results.

Many evenings, after Chase had practiced, they'd talked about their future while sitting in the bleachers. Those were the days when they were giddy with their love for each other, turning up their noses to life's realities. Back then, nothing seemed to be an obstacle. At least where Chase was concerned. She'd listened to his aspirations, bursting with confidence to be the world's best sprinter. Then she hadn't been in his life for his only Olympic experience. She could only imagine how his dreams and expectations skyrocketed.

From the sidelines, she witnessed his popularity soar. Even though they had gone their separate ways, she couldn't eliminate him completely. Endorsements paved the rapid path to his superstardom. He popped up in various advertisements featuring sports drinks, underwear, designer suits and even a mobile phone where he was calling his sweetheart to propose on camera. That ad she could do without seeing.

"What brings you here?" Chase asked.

"I might ask the same of you," Laura replied.

"Last I knew, you'd thought about following in your brother's footsteps to be a doctor."

Laura shrugged. It was one of many career options that fizzled. Sounded good until she took a look at the curriculum.

"Not to say that I'm not glad for the career switch. Gives us a chance to visit some unfinished business."

Laura shrugged again. His tentative offer taunted her, trying to lead her down a path that she didn't want to go. Guess he wasn't going to act as if they didn't have a past. Good for him. Didn't change much with her, though.

"After I tore a tendon in the world games and couldn't heal enough to make the last Olympic trials, I had to make a decision. The window was sliding shut on me," he stated with a matter-of-factness.

A slight change in his voice alerted her. She detected bitterness, maybe even remorse. His pain must hit him deeply for him to display those emotions with her.

"Don't count yourself out of the race," she advised, fighting the natural urge to put her arm around him.

"Always the optimist, right? May not have appreciated it, but it's nice to hear. I didn't count myself out. My body quit on me." He sucked in his breath and exhaled with a heavy sigh. "A decision had to be made. I quit."

"You retired."

Chase shrugged off her correction. A class jogged around the field, his gaze followed their progress.

"Are you in a lot of pain?" Silly question, but she didn't want him to open the subject and now close the shutters around it.

"Somewhat. Guess I'm turning into my grandfather who could tell when rain was coming because his knees ached. Actually, I was dead on with my prediction last Wednesday when we had that thunderstorm." He grinned, adding a teasing wink.

They had emerged on to the track field.

"Wow!" Laura exclaimed.

The stadium had groups of various athletes probably divided into their class sessions. For Laura, many hours waiting for Chase were spent seeing the good and bad with the male athletic egos, aggressive coaches and the many girlfriends. Unfortunately, many of those relationships didn't survive. Multi-tasking wasn't a priority.

Chase had focused on what was important. She'd helped him, until he no longer wanted her help. She had to accept the sacrifice to walk away.

A coed class noisily jogged past them. Some of the sweat suits had the lacrosse team logo printed down the leg. Two stragglers brought up the rear, earning them a very vocal reprimand from the coach. Yep, she had witnessed those heated discussions with Chase and his coach. She wondered if he'd felt pressure to retire, rather than lose his ranking.

A flock of birds in arrow shaped formation noisily flew past them. Laura looked up at the sky, shielding her eyes in the process. She followed them until they disappeared from view.

"What?" she asked, flustered to catch him staring at her.

"Nothing." He shoved his hands in his pocket and kicked at the gravel. "Getting used to seeing you."

Laura led the way to the bleachers. Chase sat beside her. Her pulse jogged a few beats faster. Thankfully, he left several inches of space between them. Otherwise she'd have to slide away from him for sanity's sake. Regardless of what her mind logically concluded, her heart had a tendency to be weak. There was no need to test that with any casual contact of body parts. She touted her emotional strength, but she wasn't that strong.

"Don't want you to feel uncomfortable around me," Chase spoke, his gaze fastened straight ahead.

"Shouldn't be a problem. You've got your job and I've got mine."

"Mind sticking around after hours so the team can meet you?" Chase asked.

Laura pretended to mull over the request. Let's see. She had to go to the grocery store, head home and whip up her one-person meal, then catch the latest reality show. Boring. "Sure."

"Great. Let's head back. I'll take you over to your area." He looked at his watch. "Folks should be heading out to lunch in a few minutes. Maybe we can catch a few of them. It'll be a good bonding time for you."

They walked back to the building, down the long corridors where students milled. The various halls and offices had a honeycomb effect. She envisioned several instances where she'd be wandering the halls looking for the correct office.

Chase stopped in front of an open door. "Since we're now at my office, I want to give you something."

They walked in large area room where the receptionist desk stood as the gateway to various offices on either side. The block of offices and rooms housed the department of the entire coaching staff. One wall held the various bulletin boards all covered with colored papers announcing the meets, university information and other official news.

Laura stopped near the receptionist desk. She could see into Chase's office, which wasn't more than a closet.

"I'll get it," he said before entering his office.

Chase wanted to re-think the birthday gift. His imagination had failed him, making him believe that giving a gift to an ex-girlfriend who happened to be working for him was normal. As he approached Laura and saw the suspicion cloud her face, he felt ridiculous. All he could do was act as if this was no big deal.

"I know that I'm a day late, but I think it still counts. Happy Birthday." He handed the box to her. Although shock registered, he noted the smile that tugged at her mouth.

"I don't know what to say." She shook her head. Her eyes lifted from the box to his face. "Why?" She shook her head again before accepting the box. "Thank you."

Chase didn't mind her bewilderment. He anticipated that his thoughtfulness would be unexpected. What he hoped against was her rejection of the gift. Not that it would deter him. He'd simply have to move to Plan B, whatever that happened to be.

"Should I open it now?" She held the box on her outstretched palm.

"Sure. It won't blow up." He attempted to lighten the moment. Thank goodness Sandy had left for lunch. He didn't want to make a fool of himself in front of his secretary.

He watched her pull off the ribbon around the box. Then she took a deep breath and removed the lid.

"Lots of shredded stuff," she remarked.

"Kinda grabbed it out of the shredded paper in the back."

She handed the wad of paper to him. "Well, I guess you'd better get the secrets back before you're prosecuted for espionage."

Their fingers grazed each other. Yet he wanted to repeat the motion again. He wanted to feel her long fingers, warm and soft, sliding over his hand.

"Chase! You shouldn't have."

He looked at her face closely to see if, despite her words, she did like it. Her flat statement telling him that he shouldn't have, matched her unwavering gaze, as in he really shouldn't have. Of all the responses, this was not in the top list.

A delicate gold charm bracelet with three charms dangled from her fingers where it lightly rested. Gold tiny loops formed the bracelet. He'd initially seen the piece at a Costa Rican jewelry shop while on vacation six months ago. When he'd stopped to admire it Laura came to mind because of her slight obsession with charms.

"I do think it's absolutely beautiful." Laura sighed. "But…this is a bit much. First, seeing you. Working for you so unexpectedly. Now this." She bit her lip, frowning deeply at the jewelry. She laid the bracelet on her palm and turned each charm flat against her palm.

"I remembered how much you liked unicorns." He saw the small nod when he mentioned the first charm. "And you wanted to go to Trinidad for their Carnival." Her finger traced the distinctive shape of the small Caribbean island. "Do you recognize the third?"

She stared down at the last charm. Her finger hovered above the tiny shape. Voices approached from down the hall. Classes had been dismissed and the halls filled with students and teachers. He didn't have much time left.

The third charm was a treasure chest. He looked at her face willing her to say something, anything. Could their childhood adventures with pirates, kidnapping and all out war resonate with her as it did with him? Or maybe it was the kiss that she demanded from him as ransom for his GI Joe action figure during one summer afternoon. She had shoved her girlish tendencies aside when she and Chase had played. When they were young, she had always declared herself to be the pirate.

"I recognize it."

"Don't give it back. It would mean a lot to me if you'd keep it." He placed his hand under her open palm and gently closed her fingers over the bracelet.

"I know that you've put a lot of thought into this. I also think that you knew I would be here. Otherwise, you wouldn't have given it to me. I'm not sure where you are in your life or what problems may be plaguing you. But you can't expect me to fill in the hole," she remarked, her voice hardening.

"I'm not trying to buy your affection. Friends wouldn't do that to each other."

"Take it back." Her voice shook slightly, but her eyes were clear of any tears. She pulled her hand from his and dropped the bracelet in his shirt pocket. "When I took a job here, it was because this was my goal after I got my physical therapist certificate. I'm here to work. I want nothing more from this. You're now my boss, and I want nothing but an employee-boss relationship. Anything more or anything less and I'll have to find another job."

After Laura had long disappeared down the hall and around the corner, Chase only had her lingering, gentle scent and the memory of touching her hand to keep him company.

Chapter 2

Laura didn't go out of her way to avoid contact with Chase. She didn't have to. She had full days of completing therapeutic massages and daily reports for each athlete. Three weeks after her start, she continued to feel that her decision to pursue physical therapy was the right move—even if she *was* working for Chase. Any free time or breaks were spent with her coworkers, getting to know them.

Occasionally, she did catch a glimpse of Chase as he coached the track team on her way home. The main street narrowly snaked through the campus, linking several side roads into a network of roads. Laura had no problem driving at the posted low speed limit because it allowed her to see him at work unnoticed. She figured watching him was safer.

From all the signs, Chase seemed to be honoring her wishes and leaving her alone. She still wanted to know how he knew that she'd be working there. What man walked around with a birthday gift for an ex-girlfriend waiting for the appropriate moment?

One thing was clear, he'd thought about her. She'd never admit it to him, but he'd touched her very deeply with such a thoughtful gift. His act had rattled her defenses. She couldn't deny the warm tingle that had seeped in between the cracks in her armor.

Determined to keep Chase from invading her thoughts any further, she accepted her coworker's invitation to go to happy hour at a local bar and then head to a club in downtown Atlanta. She couldn't remember the last time that she'd gone dancing.

She wanted to freshen up instead of going right

after work. She raced home, mainly taking side roads to avoid most of the traffic. A half hour later, she'd showered and dressed. Satisfied with her makeup she fluffed her hair out after wearing her usual pony-tail. However, she wasn't satisfied with her clothes. She looked bland.

She selected gold coiled drop earrings. They dangled boldly from her ear lobes. The bronze-gold color mixture stood out against the silk black shirt with tiny gold threads.

"What the heck am I doing?" she questioned the mirror. A yawn overcame her, to which she noisily succumbed. She peered into the mirror. "What a poor excuse for a party girl."

She hadn't dated much since breaking up with Chase. Who could blame her? Rejection stung. Not only had Chase's family told her that she wasn't up to par, Chase grew increasingly critical of her. It all coincided with his meteoric rise on campus, then at the state championship.

She slipped on a sensible pair of black flats. The wide shaped front made her feet look like square blocks. She frowned debating on what to do next.

A car horn honked. A few seconds later, her cell phone rang.

"Hey, Kasey." Laura walked over to the living room and pulled back the curtains, spying her friend's red Jeep below. "I'll be right down."

"Hurry up," Kasey yelled her response. She hit the annoying horn to punctuate the order.

Laura grinned. Kasey was the most outgoing and happy person that she'd met on the job. Her stories of her crazy weekends left Laura feeling a bit envious. All she could talk about of her weekends were the cable movies she watched.

She looked down at her feet once more. With an irritated grunt, she kicked off her shoes. "Darn it, life is too short." She pulled out a three inch heeled pair of mules. Turning from one side to the other in front of the mirror, she gave a somewhat satisfied grunt. She glided her hands down the sides of her hips frowning at the inches that seemed to expand on a daily basis. Maybe the black jeans in a darkened room would help mute the imperfections.

Another honk sounded. She flicked off the light switch and hurried out of her apartment.

"Looking good. You know how to clean up." Kasey grinned at her. Her loud perfume matched her loud voice and her equally loud personality.

But it was all good. Laura returned her grin and settled in the car.

"First stop is The Inner Circle," Kasey announced.

"Sounds very exclusive." Laura worried that maybe she'd underdressed. Looking at her friend and comparing outfits, Laura imagined that she'd be the Pollyanna-type next to Kasey's exposed assets.

"Tonight the club's only open to the staff, that's about it. Most of the staff hangs out there before we go our separate ways. But there's also a few other companies in the area that come to see who is our fresh meat. Can't complain, though. We do the same with their people." Kasey leaned over and squeezed her hand. "Can't wait to show you off."

"Look, I'm only hanging out. Mainly because you insisted," Laura protested. "I'm not looking for a man."

"These days, no one looks for a man." Kasey impatiently honked at the car in front that didn't pull off a second after the light turned green. "This is the age where we sample the goods, but don't stay for the feast."

"Well, I'm not hungry."

Kasey laughed. Laura couldn't help smiling. She suspected that her friendship with Kasey would be full of adventures. She hoped that she had the stamina to keep up with her.

They pulled into the parking lot, which looked fairly full. Most of the nearby parking spots were gone with only handicapped spaces available. Kasey parked between two mini-vans. Then she reached into the glove compartment and pulled out a blue hanging handicapped sign. She hooked it on the rear view mirror gave Laura a wide smile and exited.

"Kasey, you're not handicapped!"

"I know. It's my mother's. When I go out at night I use it. Figure it's safer to park near the entrances to the clubs." Kasey strutted off in her tight-fitting scooped-neck T-shirt and jeans that looked two sizes too small.

"Kasey, you can't park here!"

Kasey didn't turn around and was at the entrance.

Laura ran after her. "Give me the keys, then. I'll park it."

Kasey tossed the keys to her and disappeared through the doors.

"What a wench," Laura muttered.

She got into the car and drove around to the side where there were several open spaces. She didn't care if Kasey was irritated by her citizen-of-the-year performance a few seconds ago. If she didn't move the car, she'd think about some person with physical challenges struggling to get into the bar while she and her friend, whooped it up inside.

Unfortunately, she knew all too well what it was like to be considered less than normal.

"Laura?"

Laura recognized the smooth tone that used to call her endearments like *pretty lady, sexy brown eyes* and her personal favorite, *sweet buns*. Her cheeks warmed. Thank goodness for the cool evening.

"Glad to see you've discovered our favorite watering hole." Chase caught up to her near the doorway.

"Kasey invited me," Laura explained. She touched her hair, hoping that there were no stray strands poking up in the air.

They entered the darkened interior. Laura waited a few seconds for her eyes to adjust. She didn't need to bother.

"Laura! Chase! Over here." Kasey stood on a chair, holding a bottle of beer. She waved at them as if they were a hundred feet away.

"Hey, guys," Chase responded. His voice had changed into a low boom that made her jump. "Look who I found wandering outside."

Laura glared at Chase, not appreciating being the object of his joke.

"Introductions, please." A young man hit his empty glass repeatedly on the counter. "I'm liking what I'm seeing."

"Hold your horses, Brandon," Chase responded. "Everybody, this is Laura Masterson."

The responding greetings came back to her like an echo. Then they went around the table sharing their names. Some she recognized, but some didn't work with at the university. The young man who'd smiled like a kid in a candy shop perked up like a spaniel when it was his turn.

"Brandon Littlejohn, computer whiz extraordinaire. I work with the brokerage firm about ten minutes away." His voice carried a thick layer of boastfulness.

At first, he seemed cute and harmless. But with one drink thrown back and another one quickly ordered, Laura wondered if she was going to be stuck with his unwanted attention.

"Don't worry, I've got your back," Chase whispered in her ear. His breath tickled her ear. "And what a lovely back it is."

At twenty-six years old, she blushed. So he would still take it there. Whatever *it* was. She couldn't define what he did to her, how his words could make her emotions swirl like the beginning of a wind storm. On the other hand, his words could also cause a freeze. That, she didn't care for.

"Whoa, sweetie, I didn't mean to anger you."

Laura pulled her hair back around her ear. She accepted her drink from the waitress, taking a deep sip of cola as if it had the properties to dull her senses. She wanted more than dulling of the senses, she wanted total numbness.

"Keep it up and I'll switch chairs," Laura threatened. The only seat available happened to be next to Brandon. On one side was the geek who thought he was Casanova. On the other side, a remarkable physical specimen who once had been her Casanova.

"I won't tease you anymore." He smiled and touched his hand to his heart.

"Apology accepted."

"How's work?"

She nodded, glad for the switch in subjects.

"Getting the hang of things?" he asked.

"Going pretty good. Can't complain."

"How's the kid with the stress fracture?"

"Hey, you two, no shop talk," Kasey shouted from across the table. Her edict was followed by several kernels of popped corn being tossed at Laura and Chase.

They ducked trying to miss Kasey's accurate aim. They only succeeded in bumping heads.

"Ouch. Good gosh, you've got a hard noggin." Laura rubbed her forehead wincing at the sore spot.

"Let me have a look." He promptly grabbed her face in his hands. "Whoa. Are you going to look a sight tomorrow," he whistled.

Laura jerked her head away from Chase's hand. Her body responded, recognizing the trigger that caused a physical reaction that had nothing to do with extreme temperatures. A warm flush blossomed from her cheeks, where his hands only a few seconds ago pressed against her face, and now ran through her body.

"You know, you don't have to be afraid of me." Chase looked perplexed.

"I know. I'm not."

"Could have fooled me." Chase drained his glass and set it down with a firm tap.

"Look, Chase, I don't understand why we're suddenly in each other's space. You've moved on and so have I." At least she was trying to move on and not think about him. Now that she worked in the same building and *for* him, her emotional separation threatened to evaporate.

"Hey, you two," Kasey shouted across the table. "Looking awfully serious." She and few others shared a laugh at their expense.

"Laura is an old friend from my hometown in Maryland," Chase explained.

Laura saw the sudden gleam in Kasey's eyes as she glanced at him and then at her. To her horror, Kasey picked up her drink and practically ran over to them.

"Laura, some friend you are." Kasey playfully punched Laura in the arm. "How could you keep this from me? To the famous Chase Westfield and Laura Masterson." She grinned, her face looked as if she would burst before she had the first opportunity to tell the news.

"It was a long time ago." Laura didn't bother to look at Chase, not caring what his version would be.

"Looks like there may be some spark left." Kasey signaled the waiter over and ordered another round. "Get this one a chardonnay, instead of a cola."

Laura shook her head. "Cola, please." She had a feeling that she'd be driving Kasey home. Now that her friend was getting comfortable, they probably weren't going to the club. This change in plans suited her. As a matter of fact, she'd rather leave now to head home.

None of them spoke. Music blared. People poured in. The bar had gotten lively. And then the karaoke singing began. Laura seized the noisy distraction to grab her soda and head for an empty seat near the stage.

Soon she was laughing as a young man attempted to sing an Earth, Wind and Fire song. His attempt at the falsetto had her doubled over with tears rolling down her cheeks. Only after he'd left did she notice Kasey sitting next to her. She didn't want to look for Chase, but did wonder where he'd disappeared to.

"I can see why you jumped on that." Kasey slurped her drink. Laura knew it had to be at least the fourth or even fifth drink.

"Jumped on what?" Laura shot back, as if she didn't know.

"I'd heard he wasn't bad to look at, but up close, he's good gosh almighty—darned beautiful." Kasey laughed at her own comments.

Laura shrugged, knowing that her friend would be like a dog with a juicy bone.

Another wannabe-singer walked on to the stage and decided on a Mariah Carey song. During her butchering of a perfectly fine song, the crowd who had gotten into the swing showed no mercy. By the time the poor woman had ended, the crowd had split between full laughter and boos. Laura could never boo anyone, so she opted for the side-splitting laughter. She'd feel guilty later.

"Speak of the devil." Kasey nudged her.

"What?" Laura looked over at Kasey, then followed her gaze. Chase stood on the stage.

What the heck was he doing up there? Chase may have been a spokesman for various products and used to cameras and fans, but voluntarily having the spotlight was so not him.

"Didn't know he could sing. My, but this is a night filled with discoveries." Kasey slurped her drink.

"For me, too," Laura muttered under her breath. She settled back in the chair. There would be no laughing and certainly no booing. Chase had a voice that could've landed him a record contract if that was his passion. She glanced around for the waiter, deciding that she might need something stronger, after all.

"Ladies and gentlemen," Chase began. "I'd like throw a little old-school out at you."

A roar went up from the crowd. Great. He won them over with no problem. When did he become such a ham? Back in the day, he only sang in church and once at his mother's birthday.

"But first, I need my partner in crime with me. We never actually sang this, but we did roller skate to it when we were kids."

Laura stared. Then set her glass down to flee. She couldn't believe that Chase had the nerve to spread this insanity to her. Well, she wasn't playing.

"Folks, I think my other half is leaving. Don't

you want to hear that classic hit, *Reunited,* by Peaches and Herb? Come on folks, let Laura know that you care."

Laura heard her name being thrown back at her like an annoying echo. Someone reached for her elbow, yanking her back so that she lost her footing.

"Get your hands off me." Laura glared at the man who had too much to drink. She pushed away from him, as he hooted and hollered with his friends. She turned to look at Chase who still called her up to the stage to join him.

Anger propelled her forward. She'd had enough. With or without Kasey, she was leaving. But before she left, she planned to tell Chase and his alter ego just what she thought of his school boy antics.

Laura strode up to Chase, stopping a few inches from his face. Her finger started poking at his chest before she could think straight to get out the words.

He smiled with all his teeth and charm displayed, while she sputtered incoherently. Why did he have to look so good? Never mind that, she knew enough to stop talking when he shoved the microphone in front of her.

The music started. Then the words scrolled on the monitor. Chase put his arms around her waist. He held firm. With a bold wink, he pulled her into his arms, swaying to the music. Laura looked out at the crowd, deciding not to make a scene. Plus the song was so addictive that her brain already followed the lyrics, reminding her of their times in the roller skating rink.

As a teenager, she couldn't wait for couples only. He'd come to take her hand while she was surrounded by her girlfriends. They would descend into a giggling mess, while she left them for Chase. They'd skate hand-in-hand, weaving their way among the others, each wrapped up in their own world.

She may not have been allowed to go on dates, but the skating rink was as good as alone time. Her siblings had to attend and so did his sister. But everyone was on the prowl to hook up with someone, so no one bothered her and Chase. Besides, everyone took it for granted that they were together.

She sang the words, knowing that she wasn't

anywhere close to the quality of Chase's melodious voice. Although she sensed him looking down at her, she refused to look into his eyes. He already had enough power over to her to make her act like a fool for four minutes. She didn't need her legs to feel like rubber when she gazed into his honey brown eyes.

The song did manage to summarize some of her feelings and the current state of affairs with this sudden reunion. Boy, did it feel good to lean against his body, firm and very muscular. His hand sliding up and down her back made her want to purr. She was relaxed enough to sway in time with him. Her leg slipped between his as they waltzed the last verse.

Her brother, Pierce, had taught her to dance the box step. But Chase had taken it to another level full of sensuality and forbidden passion. When he spun her and ended the move with a dip, she succumbed and slowly moved her gaze from his full lips in its constant grin, up to his nose with its slender bridge, up to his eyes that pierced her with their intensity.

The song died and yet she remained in his arms. Good sense prevailed as she broke the eye

contact. Or, maybe it was Kasey's sudden appearance as she popped her head between theirs.

"That was awesome, guys. Ever thought about
taking that stuff on the road?" Kasey straightened
up and emitted a loud hiccup. "You all shouldn't
break up. Ya'll look too good together."

Laura stepped away from Chase. Any high that
she could've blamed on the caffeine from the cola
was gone. There'd be no getting together. His
family had made sure of that and he had aided and
abetted everyone's handiwork.

Maturity had given her an upper hand. She
didn't plan to be in the position where a man's rejection could devastate her to that degree. Life
may not have any guarantees, but it didn't mean
that she had to go blindly into wrong situations.

"Kasey, I'm ready to go." Based on her friend's
drunken weave back to the chair, Laura figured
that Kasey needed to leave also.

"What's the rush?" Kasey asked, her voice
slurred.

"You're right, you should get her home. Do
you need any help?"

Laura jumped, not realizing that he'd approached.

"I'm fine." Kasey stomped her foot. The effort threw her off balance and she fell heavily into a nearby chair.

Laura didn't want to make a scene. She hoped that her friend would follow her quietly to the car. Despite the fact that she really wanted to get out of there and put some distance between Chase and herself, she couldn't in good conscience leave Kasey. She'd never forgive herself, if something happened.

"I don't need your help." Kasey showed her annoyance by shoving a chair aside before Laura clamped a tight, firm grip around her friend's waist and propelled her out of the building.

Immediately the cool night air hit them with a shocking blast. It had the desired effect, letting some rational thought make headway this disastrous night. She snapped the seat belt around Kasey.

A tap on the glass startled her. Her nerves were on edge.

Chase motioned for her to lower the window. She started the car first just to let him know that there would be no long conversations. Then she pushed the black button on the door panel until the window slid down mid-point.

"I can follow so you can leave her car at her place. Then I can give you a ride home."

"Nope." She hadn't thought about the car logistics, unless she took Kasey to her place.

"Laura, I know that I'm fine enough to drive." Kasey must have seen the ready argument on Laura's face. "But let's go home. I've got to head to Savannah tomorrow morning—early."

"And you were out partying tonight?" Gosh, she sounded like her mother.

"Well, I roll like that." Kasey yawned and leaned her head back on the head rest.

"If you ask me, I don't think she's going to be fit to go anywhere until probably noon tomorrow," Chase offered.

Laura nodded, keeping her eyes forward. To turn her head would mean that he was in kissable distance. Thanks to Kasey's SUV, she was sitting high enough that she or he only had to lean forward and succumb to a good night smooch.

Not a chance.

"For once, would you not be so stubborn?" Chase placed his forearms on the door.

"Stubborn? Because I won't let you take me home?"

He pulled on his ear lobe, a familiar habit when he got irritated. *Good*. His cologne was driving her crazy. The very clear memory of swaying to an old-school song had more than her mind buzzing. And darn it, she couldn't stop thinking about kissing him.

Maybe that's why she turned her head. Of course, she later told herself that she had to let him know whom he was dealing with, eye-to-eye.

"We're not buddies, Chase. I need this favor from you to take me home. But don't think what happened in there is the beginning of a new chapter for us. We are still at the end of the happy trail. No happily ever after, no riding off into the sunset and certainly no reunion of the cast members here." She had more to say about hurt and disappointment, but for the life of her, she couldn't remember what it was. But she shouldn't have looked into his eyes.

Then, she made the mistake of looking at that mouth. The perfect mouth that Pierce had taken pleasure in punching when he caught them kissing behind the large oak tree in Chase's backyard. At fourteen years old, the kiss was a mere peck, but she swore that she'd floated up past the trees, over the neighborhood to settle among the clouds.

In college, and after college, their relationship had moved beyond chaste, stolen moments. Chase could make her melt into an incoherent puddle when she was locked in his arms for a steamy kiss after a rousing night of passionate lovemaking.

"Have dinner with me."

"Did you hear anything I just said?" Laura couldn't believe his tenacity.

"Yes. And if you have dinner with me, I'll clear up all the questions."

She could demand that he cleared them up now. Who was he to give her conditions after all he'd made her go through?

"It's cold and I'm freezing my buns out here," he complained.

His buns weren't bad either. Sprinter buns.

"Fine." She pursed her lips, detecting an amused twitch to his mouth. "Don't think you've landed some big coup. I'm on to you, Chase West-field."

"Good, then you'll know that I've wanted to do this since I saw you." He leaned in and covered her mouth with his. He didn't touch her, didn't pin her face between his hands, did nothing to force her to be kissed. Yet, like a magnet, she couldn't pull away drawn by an intangible force that ignited when they were together.

His attention was gentle, loving, coaxing for which she obliged his attentive tongue. Her entire body tingled, aroused out of a deep slumber, yearning for fulfillment.

He pulled away first. Laura opened her eyes, unable to speak. Only her chest rose and fell with an uneven breath.

"Let's get you home, shall we?" Chase jingled his keys and turned to head to his car.

"That son of a—" Laura called out.

"Girl, shut your mouth. He lit you up like a Christmas tree," Kasey uttered and promptly fell asleep with a small snore escaping.

Chapter 3

By the time Laura drove to Kasey's apartment, there was no way she would be able to drag her drunken, sleepy form out of the SUV, down the path to the building and then up the stairs to the top floor. She shook her friend's shoulder in a futile last attempt.

Chase tapped at Kasey's window, motioning for her to unlock the door. Laura complied, not having much choice. She'd need his muscle to heft her coworker's tall frame.

Together they made slow progress. Sometimes

Kasey did revive long enough to actually walk before teetering over. They escorted her to the bedroom and gently laid her down. Chase excused himself so Laura could tend to Kasey's clothing. When she was done undressing her, she pulled the floral printed comforter over her body. Then she turned out the light and left the bedroom door partially open.

"Chase, I really don't feel comfortable leaving her in this condition." Laura turned to look at the door. "What if she gets sick and can't get up?"

"I'm inclined to agree with you."

"You go ahead, I can call a cab in the morning," she said.

"Or I can stay here with you."

Laura shook her head. Chase may think he was in control, playing games with her by seducing her, but she still had the good sense to say no.

To show him that she did have strength, she walked past him and opened the apartment door. "I've got this under control."

He looked as if he was about to object, then reconsidered. "Okay." He looked at her, shoving his hands deep into his pockets. As he walked past her, he paused without turning around.

"Yes?" She wished that her voice didn't sound so needy.

"I can expect you for dinner tomorrow, right?"

"Yes," she answered.

"Good." He pulled the door closed behind him.

Laura stood there staring at the door, wondering how her life could have taken such a sudden shift. Not that she had ever stopped thinking about Chase, but she certainly didn't entertain any ideas that they would be talking, much less having dinner.

Well, so much for the late night at the club. Guess she was in for the night. Seems like no matter what she did, she was always in for the night. This time she didn't mind so much. She flopped on the couch, reached for the remote and slid into a comfortable position.

"Who's the latest dish waiting to be served?"

Chase looked up from stirring the Alfredo sauce. "Deon, you need to be out of here in five minutes."

"Only came to return your toolkit. Not planning to cramp your style." His friend inhaled, patting his stomach for emphasis. "A brother could do with a little bite before facing the cold."

"You're not staying." Chased moved the pot off the stove. He'd hate to burn the sauce after every other part of the four-course meal met with his level of perfection. "Besides, I'm sure Chantal, Sarita, Bonnie or whoever the latest is wants you in the sex cave next door."

"They are all has-beens, like I've been preaching to you, man. You've got to change the girls as often as you change your shoes." His old teammate Deon was known for donating his running shoes after each meet.

"Well, now that I'm an old man, injuries and all, got to make do with whatever I can." Chase walked over to Deon, grabbed him by the elbow and escorted him toward the door.

"Usually I get to meet them," Deon complained.

"Only the ones that you insist on introducing to me. And frankly, they are never my type."

"You don't have a type. I've brought tall, short, fat, skinny, dark skinned and even light-bright. Nothing. I was thinking that I'd have to get a girlie magazine for you to see if you got it going on."

Chase laughed at Deon's silliness. He'd seen the women at the clubs with whom Deon strutted, and knew his friend belonged in the dog pound. None of his so-called women made it in his company in daylight hours because they weren't the sort you'd take home to mother.

The few times that he'd given into Deon's blind dating tactics, he'd regretted the waste of his time. Aggressive women didn't necessarily turn him off, but he did want the feelings to be mutual. He wanted to at least feel some kind of snap, crackle or pop when he was in their presence. Instead, he found himself thinking of mundane tasks like taking out the recyclables for the next day's pick-up.

Deon finally gave up and left.

With Deon out of the way, Chase returned to cooking. He still had time to set the table and add the finishing touches to the room. He couldn't control the mood in the workplace, but his house was a different story. Having Laura over for dinner hadn't been planned. The invite had popped into his head when he stood mere inches from her that night at the bar. Now that his initial fear of a scene at their first meeting was over, he could relax.

From her fine features and slender neck to the

dark sweep of her hair, he wanted to be near her. In a sweeping bit of nostalgia, he wanted to feel her lips against his. Her earlier response couldn't have been a figment of his imagination.

As he lit the thick vanilla scented candles, he thought about the flame in his heart that would never go out for Laura. Not many people got a chance to have a do-over in life. He could only hope that Laura would give him that chance.

Half an hour later, with a soft smell of the sweet spice filling the air, Chase surveyed the dining table with its setting for two. Then he turned his attention to the living room where the candles of various heights dotted the room. On the center piece table was a bowl of assorted roses with stems cut short, making the arrangement look thick and colorful. He'd ordered the vibrant array of colors off the Internet to cut the monotonous brown shade of his couch and furniture. It paid to watch a few of the popular interior designing shows.

His phone rang. His spirit dropped, thinking that it had to be Laura canceling. His disappointment waited in limbo as he picked up the receiver. "Yes?"

"Chase, it's Laura. Sorry, I'm running late. I left the directions at home and thought that I could rely on memory." She laughed. "Wrong move."

Chase shoved the disappointment back down with a big sense of relief. She was on her way. "No problem." He provided the directions, impressed that she'd made it into his neighborhood, two streets away.

He went outside to greet her, knowing that she was probably a bundle of nerves after driving around the area. As an afterthought, he ran back into the house, hoping that he didn't miss her arrival. Hastily, he pulled a yellow rose out of the bowl and headed back outside.

Under the startling sunlight, he felt like a schoolboy waiting for someone to give him attention while he stood there with the flower. He stared down at the flower as if it would provide an answer.

A quick horn tap sounded and he looked up to see Laura waving from the nearby street corner. Maybe the romantic gesture would be too much. He tossed the flower in the hedge. Then he walked toward the mailbox as if that was his primary reason for being outdoors. She pulled up next to the curb offering him a quick wave.

"Hey, see that wasn't too bad," he offered.

"Yep, your directions were perfect." She approached him and offered him a bottle of wine.

He should have kept the rose. He wondered if he could reach down to retrieve it from the hedge where it landed. Instead he took the wine and pretended to read the label. "Wonderful." He had no clue about drinks. Maybe wine tasting would be the next hobby as he adjusted to his retirement phase.

He ushered her in, glad to see that she was suitably impressed with his new home. She handed her coat to him, which he took to the closet.

"Amazing." Laura's voice reflected her awe.

"It's what I like to call home." Why on earth did he sound like a good TV dad? "How's Kasey?"

"She'll survive. Right now she's making all kinds of resolutions to stop drinking." They laughed.

"Come on in. I have appetizers for us to enjoy." Chase motioned toward the living room, before heading into the kitchen. He could see her from the kitchen as he added the finishing touches to the chicken tenderloins cooked on skewers served with cucumber dip or peanut sauce.

"You went all out. Hope you're not disappointed."

"You wouldn't disappoint me," he teased.

She shrugged, a shadow flitted across her face.

"Have a seat." He set the serving dish on the table. Laura hadn't moved. He turned to see why she resisted his simple request. She was perusing the photographs and various tokens of his mastery in sports.

Not wanting to disturb her, he continued setting out the small plates and napkins. Wondering if she was in the mood for quiet or chatting, he turned on the stereo with his remote and let the CD of R&B classics play. A line up of Roberta Flack, Temptations, Stevie Wonder and Barry White couldn't hurt a candlelit dinner.

"I'm really confused," Laura spoke over her shoulder. She had looked at the framed photographs, medals, championship cups and now turned her attention on him. "You could have anything you want." She threw her arms out expansively. "Why are you here? I know Atlanta is the new Mecca for upwardly mobile African Americans, but why are *you* here? Why a college coach? I imagine that you could be a personal coach for the next up and coming athlete. Now you're bogged down with politics and the administration. This is my world, not yours."

Chase bit into the chicken on the wood skewers. He needed a minute to think. He slid the plate to Laura, glad to see that she finally thought about eating.

"My body's broken up, Laura. Maybe I'll go back to reclaim my place in the world after a year of healing. On my contracts, I still have endorsements and a few lecture circuits to hit for the coming year. I didn't plan to retire so early, but it's what had to happen."

Neither spoke.

"Do you mind if I freshen up?" Laura looked around abruptly.

"Go right ahead. Off to your right. That'll give me some time to transfer the food from the kitchen to the dining room."

"I'll help."

"Thanks, but you're not allowed to lift a finger, except to eat," he explained.

Laura acknowledged his request and aimed for

the bathroom. She closed the door, glad to get away for a few seconds. Several times she'd wanted to cancel. By not resisting Chase and that mind-blowing kiss, he could have the wrong idea that she was willing to play on dangerous ground. Then, she followed up with accepting his dinner invitation!

Laura made a face in the mirror. She smoothed her eyebrows, inspecting the rest of her face. Only her eyes and lips were made up. After a late night with light sleep, she needed the smoky eyeliner to enhance her eyes and make them look larger and more awake. With the same thought in mind, she had selected a reddish hued lipstick as a bright spot of color for liveliness.

Dishes clinked outside the room. Guess it was time to exit and face the result of her decision. She ran her fingers through her hair, tossing back the front piece so that it lay feathered on one side of her face. Enough with her fidgeting, she opened the door.

"Do you have a preference?" Chase stood behind one of the chairs, waiting for her decision.

Laura shook her head. She took the other chair, but Chase slid over to assist her. When he lightly touched her shoulder, she froze hoping that he would return to the other chair so she could breathe normally.

"Everything smells wonderful." Laura did admire the line up of dishes. She couldn't believe that his culinary skills had become so developed.

"There's a garden salad, soup and Alfredo pasta with grilled chicken breast."

"I'm embarrassed at how much you've done on my behalf."

"Don't be. Yes, I did spend a bit of time preparing, but this is my olive branch to you to keep the past in the past. Can we move forward?"

Laura took a gulp of wine, choking in the process. Over the rim of her wine glass she studied him.

"Look, Chase, I think we'd better keep this on neutral ground."

"If that'll make you feel better."

"It would." She ate her salad, enjoying the sweet, zesty vinaigrette poured lightly over the greens. "Someone made you very domesticated." No sooner had the statement escaped than she blushed at the direct hit her question made. She felt like a hypocrite calling for neutrality when she zeroed in on what occupied her thoughts—Chase with another woman.

"There were some times when I wasn't training and I wasn't playing at being a sports model. Usually, I was in a hotel room bored to death, flipping through channels. Regardless of the country, there was always a food channel. In France, I had the honor of working with a master chef in one of the major hotels. She was so appalled at my limited knowledge that she gave me a crash course in food and its preparation."

"Is that all she taught you?"

"She taught me lots of things." A soft smile touched his face.

"Sounds like she's earned a special place in your heart." Laura gritted her teeth.

"I do miss her."

"Another woman with a broken heart?"

"Jealous?" He grinned.

"No, just wondering if there are enough to form a support group."

"One sec." He pushed back the table. His amused expression irritated her. She watched him go to the bookcase and pull a photo album off the shelf. He flipped the thick pages until he came to the desired page. Marking the page with his finger, he came toward her. Curiosity prickled her. Maybe the album would explain the reason for his triumphant look.

"What?" She looked down at the page where his finger pointed.

"My darling chef."

"This doesn't mean anything. You might have been her boy toy." The little old woman had a grandmotherly smile and hair full of white curls.

"You're a sick puppy."

"Are these people her family?" Laura couldn't help being intrigued.

"Yes. Three generations, almost four. Her granddaughter was pregnant at the time." He took a deep breath, his voice a tad wistful. "She's since died. Her son and his company were my main sponsor in France and we hit it off. I got adopted by the family. Or maybe I let myself be surrounded by them."

"I'm sorry to hear of her passing. I would've loved to pass on my gratitude that you've graduated from grilled cheese sandwiches melted by your iron to a wonderful tasty meal." She wiped the corner of her mouth with the napkin, grinning at him. "And how's your family?" she asked.

"I'm sure you don't want to hear about my mother and father on an empty stomach." He opened a soup tureen. "This isn't the main dish."

"Chase, I can't eat all of this food."

"See, that's one of the things I learned in France. You shouldn't eat your food in a huge rush. It should be savored, the company enjoyed, conversation shared."

Laura followed his advice. The vegetable soup was simple and delicious. Chase kept the conversation lighthearted. By the time she had moved to the meal, her taste buds were on sensory overload. The Alfredo sauce tasted like heaven and she acknowledged with each forkful of pasta that the hips would get a little rounder and her arms may flap in the wind. It didn't stop her from chewing the large mouthful of food. She closed her eyes, enjoying the rich flavor.

"You asked about my family. Guess what, my mother asked about you when I was home recuperating."

That made her swallow before she was ready. Now the pasta stuck briefly in her throat. "What did you tell her?" she gasped.

"What could I tell her? That I hadn't seen you

in ages. That I thought about you all the time. I'd made the biggest mistake in letting you go."

"And your mother passed out, right? You almost have me convinced that I hear regret in your voice?"

"Regrets and an apology."

"You're making me nervous, Mr. Westfield. Can't believe that I'm here having a casual dinner with you."

"So I'm forgiven?"

"I didn't say all that." She didn't have to be psychoanalyzed to acknowledge that there was deep-seated anger like a thick sheet of ice far from any thaw. "Why do you care so much about getting on my good side?"

"When my parents asked about you, I talked about all your strengths. The reasons why I fell in love with you. Now that I'm facing a career switch and settling down to a another life, I began to think that there may be a chance to revive what we had. Even your family thought we would be together."

"That's an exaggeration. Omar thought you were a superhero. Pierce and Sheena were too upset by your family's treatment and gossip to feel warm and fuzzy over you." Laura put down her fork. She was full anyway and didn't want to continue eating. Did Chase forget how his mother treated her brothers and sister—not to mention her?

He could play the amnesiac. She'd never forget how his parents treated them like charity cases when her parents separated. But when Chase became interested in her beyond simple friendship, his parents' true feelings came out loud and clear. They didn't think that the Mastersons were a family that should merge with the Westfields.

"I know my family has hurt you but let me continue. After I decided to retire, I had to think about what I would do with my life. Coaching seemed like a natural tie-in. I didn't think that I'd be running a department. That opportunity fell in my lap. While I was interviewing, and that took several months, I asked about the staff. I couldn't believe my ears when I heard that you would be working on the staff and for me, no less. I even went back home to check up on what you were doing."

"You went home to Maryland?" Laura asked, not believing all of this.

"Yes, I talked to Pierce and his new wife— Haley? Even met your stepniece. Cute kid. When they confirmed that you were coming to Atlanta, I accepted the job offer."

"Just like that." Laura traced designs on the table cloth. She should be ecstatic that Chase had gone to so much trouble to locate her. Instead, she was uneasy under his focus.

Their last meeting had been ugly when Chase basically told her that he couldn't focus on both her *and* his career. He had to make the choice, which he did when he said that he was going to Europe in three days and they should use that time and separation to rethink what they wanted from each other. Laura knew what she wanted and didn't need a phony trial separation to make that determination. That had been it.

"Let's toast."

She shook her head when Chase reached for the bottle. This wasn't the time to be tipsy. Not that she felt Chase would ever take advantage of her, but poor judgment and a hungry imagination could be her demise.

Chase raised his wine glass. "To the past, present and future. And to long-lasting friendships."

She drained what little was left in her glass. "This is all a little too heavy." She pushed away from the table.

"Let's go out on the deck." He led the way through the family room off the kitchen and through a pair of French doors.

Laura inhaled deeply, mainly to clear her head. It was a bit chilly, but she didn't plan to stay out there long. As a matter of fact, she didn't plan to stay at the house much longer. It was time for her to go home and step back into reality. But first, she wanted to get a few things off her mind.

"You've got a beautiful place." The backyard didn't match the monster size house, but from the look of the neighborhood that was typical of the properties. A privacy fence enclosed the backyard where only a storage shed stood.

"I like it. Hopefully I can settle down now and raise a family," Chase said.

This was certainly a new side of Chase Westfield. "I hope you do. I think that you'll make a good father one day."

"How about a good husband?"

"I wouldn't know." Laura looked at her watch.

She really needed to leave. Get the heck out of here, far from Chase, back to her home.

Chase approached her to stand in front of her. Then he placed his hands on her shoulders. Laura tried not to meet his scrutiny, instead focusing on his right shoulder. A small shiver ran through her. She took a step back, but he matched it with a step forward. Then he took another step.

She didn't move.

His hands slid up her neck, so warm against her skin. As she turned her head to the side, her hair fell across her cheek.

"I don't think this is a good idea," Laura whispered. "I'm attracted to you, as much as I fight against it."

His hands continued their climb until he cupped her face.

Panic surged, almost choking off her airway. Laura grabbed his face and leaned her forehead against his. She closed her eyes, squeezing back the tears. "Why are you doing this?" She blew out the words in an exasperated, tearful gasp.

"I love you."

He could have slapped her. The effect would have been the same.

Laura pushed him away and returned inside the house, heading for her coat. "Buy me gifts. Kiss me. Cook dinner. Then, say you love me." She shouted the last sentence at him. If she could only see clearly through the tears to find her pocket book. A sob escaped. "What's next, Chase? How much more cruel can you be? Do you think that I'm something you put on the shelf when it doesn't fit your image? But now you're that you're retired and back with us lowly people, I'm suddenly perfect for you."

Laura's deep sadness gave way to the anger that built like an incoming tide with a monstrous wave. She pushed him away when he walked up and opened his arms. Her foot hit the pocketbook.

"Laura, I want to marry you."

Laura stopped, her hand on the door knob. She had all kinds of things to say. The promise of those words that she'd so wanted to hear four years ago was a little too late. What was so sad was that Chase didn't think that she'd have issues with his reemergence. Who did he think she was?

Laura opened the door and stepped outside. She'd done a lot of growing up in four years. She had her new career and her life ahead of her.

There was nothing more to say. She slammed the door closed behind her.

"Chase Westfield. You're a sight for sore eyes."

"Hi, Coach. Come in. Have a seat." Chase closed the door, wishing for the umpteenth time that he'd met with his coach at a restaurant, instead of his office. Nothing could remain private on a campus.

"You in a suit, behind a desk. Boy, you're going to get fat and lazy if you don't get out to the track. I know you said you needed time off to think and heal and all that gobbledygook." Coach Henderson opened his coat and settled in the chair.

Chase knew that he studied him with an expert eye as he walked and took his seat behind the desk.

"Don't go silent on me, Chase."

"I'm not. Just figured you were only beginning to get wound up."

"Don't be a smart ass." Coach leaned forward and rested his beefy arm on the desk. "Heard you haven't been going to physical therapy. As a matter of fact, no one has seen you."

"Took a break from that, too."

"You can't retire at the prime of your abilities." Henderson rubbed a hand over his head. "I'm the one that should be talking about retiring. See, I'm losing hair." He bent his head and sure enough, the thin spot had become a round bald spot with peppered gray on the sides. Chase knew better than to agree with his coach, though.

"I get that you want to retire. It scares you to have the type of injuries that you've suffered. Heck, I tore both ACLs, making the long jump and anything else I'd done a part of my history. But sheer determination and a no-quit attitude kept me going. I'm darn proud of that. I can look at myself in the mirror and know that I'm not a quitter." His coach glared at Chase.

"I hear you, Coach," Chase replied, his voice a smidgen above a whisper. He broke his coach's gaze and looked down at his steepled fingers. "I did what I set out to do. I wanted to break my school records. I did. I wanted to break college records, I did. Then it was on to the state, I broke those, too. In one case, no one has been able to break it. You know my ultimate dream was to be a part of the Olympics. I got there, even medaled."

"I know you wanted the gold," Coach reminded him. "That's what we were working for in the last Olympics."

"And then my tendon popped like a used up rubber band." Chase fought the urge to rub his heel as he remembered the excruciating pain that dropped him to his knees. Tears had stung from the hot dagger that felt as if it sliced through to the bone. Only the cameras and male pride made him suck it up.

"Chase, you're young. You were injured a year ago. Rehab techniques are fantastic. And you're a smart athlete." Coach Henderson slammed his fist on the desk.

The mad vein popped up in the middle of his forehead in a vertical line dividing east from west. Chase usually depended on that as the barometer for how furious his coach was at him. Not good.

"You young people want everything handed to you on a platter. You don't want to work for it." His coach stood and pushed back the offending chair. He pointed a long finger at him. "I've talked to the doctors. I've talked to the physical therapist. I've even talked to God about you, son. Now you look me in the eye."

Chase was already looking him in the eye. He didn't have a choice. The hypnotic effect of his coach's voice and demeanor put him in a close second to James Earl Jones.

Coach laid down his own gold Olympic medal. "Tell me that you don't want this anymore. Tell me that you're ready to hang it all up to sit behind cheap furniture and push papers."

From the growing paper stacks on his desk, Chase felt that Coach had basically summed up his job, accurately. The old man definitely played dirty, dangling that symbol of achievement in front of him. His coach knew how painful it was for him to have to admit defeat.

"I've got new kids signing on for me to coach them. I know they use your success, Chase, to define my success as a coach. They all want me to perform miracles. But no one has come with that special something that I saw in you from the first day." He put on his coat and buttoned it up. "Lie to yourself if you want to. I can see the devil do its dance in your eyes. Where's your heart?" He thumped his chest and turned to head for the door.

"Nice to see you, Coach."

His coach raised a hand, but said nothing as he exited his office.

Chase uttered a frustrated groan, then hurried after him.

They were outside walking next to the building heading to the parking lot. Of course, the track field was in full view.

"I hear everything that you're saying. Yes, I'm not going to lie, not having the gold medal hurts. But in the whole scheme of things, it's not the end of the world."

His coach almost tripped. Chase offered a steady hand, which was brushed away.

"While I was lying in the hospital and then in my apartment, I realized that I'm only as good as my last accomplishment. People forget who you are. They don't really care what I think or believe. I'm a commodity. Now I'm doing things for me. I don't know how long I'll be here in this job, but I want a normal life," Chase explained, still wanting his coach's understanding.

"Who are you talking to?" They had reached his coach's car. He opened his door and paused, leaning against the top of the car. "You sound as if you trying to convince yourself in front of a review board. I know your body is ready for the track again, even if your heart isn't willing. I'm no fool."

Chase wanted to defend himself against his coach's disappointment, against his very own doubts. He had other reasons for turning his back on rekindling his career. The one person who mattered had spurned him. But it didn't matter. He would sacrifice whatever he had to have Laura back in his life even if it meant turning his back on being a world-class sprinter.

"I'll be saying my good-byes, now. I've said all that I had to say. But you think about it. Opportunities don't usually knock twice."

"Exactly." Chase stared at his coach's car drive away. He rocked forward on his heel, took a deep breath and turned to look at his new place of employment.

A large, square red brick building with classical white columns and moldings. Institutional. Solid. Normal. Caged.

But running around a track couldn't be his life's only ambition. He had enough money to live comfortably. Living the remainder of his life on a couch, looking at photos of his past, wasn't his thing. Plus it seemed too darned lonely. He'd a lot to be ashamed for. One thing was for sure, he'd prove life wrong, that he could have a second chance. His heart told him so, now to convince Laura.

Chapter 4

"The football team is a wicked bunch."

Laura looked up from her paperwork. Kasey, her coworker, peered through the window blinds. In the first week, she'd come to realize that Kasey didn't care for the administrative part of the job. Instead, she preferred working with students, chatting and laughing over their exploits. Then she spent long hours playing catch up with her memory and the paper work.

"You need to stop looking at those young 'uns.

And what would Ray think if he knew you were ready to rob the cradle?"

Kasey glared at her and sucked her teeth. "There is no Ray. I'm done with that fool. Caught him in lie number forty-three."

"Only two days ago he sent you flowers and the adorable stuffed bear."

"Don't remind me." Kasey's face crumpled, her eyes welling with tears. She turned toward the window, resuming her watch. "The gifts were for a guilty conscience."

"You have proof? Or are you guessing? Did he confess?" Laura thought she was impulsive, until she met Kasey.

"I had a dream." Kasey shook her head. "I know it's true."

Laura frowned. Not that she considered herself an expert on relationships, but she thought that Ray may deserve more than his girlfriend's current feelings. "I think you need to be sure before ending something that you obviously treasure." How many times had she heard the great virtues of Ray, even when she could have done without more of the graphic, sexual nature of his virtues?

"Fine. I'll tell you what happened. His girl-friend of two years told me."

"Could be a jealous woman who wants your man," Laura defended. Ray seemed like a nice guy. Why'd he have to be a schmuck?

"She helped pick out the bear."

Laura opened her mouth for a quick response, but had to close it because words truly failed her. Her mind felt as if it was stuck in some type of hovering pattern, circling the wreckage that was about to be revealed.

Kasey walked away from the window and took her seat at the desk next to Laura's. Her cheeks glistened. Laura pulled out a couple tissues and handed them to her. Her coworker blew her nose noisily and tossed the tissue.

"Ray is definitely out of my life." She sniffed. "Now I'm strictly only sight-seeing. Sooner or later, a man will hurt you. Take my advice, don't let your heart take over."

Laura hoped that the shock from Kasey's change of heart didn't register on her face. She could always depend on Kasey to be dramatic about her love life with the romantic abandon of a teenager. Her friend provided a stark opposite to her opinion on men and commitment. Now with this swift change of direction, there was no balance. They both couldn't buy into the notion that the only thing men were good for were getting rid of creepy bugs.

"Ladies, how are things in here? Seems to be a lot of chatter." Gladys Newton, her immediate supervisor, stood in the doorway, casting a disdainful eye over the room.

How could one woman affect the temperature in a room? Her mere presence froze everyone into silence. Only the soft whirring sounds from the elliptical bikes could be heard. Laura prided her ability to intuitively judge someone. And what she could discern about her boss didn't sit well.

Gladys strode into the room and picked up the charts to review the notes. Kasey had wiped off the tears from her face and stood at attention as if she was being reviewed by the drill sergeant. Laura remained where she was, cleaning off the tables with the disinfectant spray and laying down clean sanitary paper. Maybe if she kept her head down and her hands busy, she wouldn't have to endure one of Gladys's examinations.

"So how are you enjoying things around here, Laura?"

Laura looked up and offered a tight smile. "Fine."

"Glad that you make good use of your time. I hate to see employees dilly dallying." She looked over at Kasey with a stern expression.

There was a knock at the entry way leading to their area. Laura looked up, finding the knocking unusual since no one knocked, not even the clients.

"Oh, Chase, coming to visit our part of the world?" Gladys chirped.

Laura not only stopped wiping the tables, but also snuck a peek to Chase's response to Gladys's syrup-laden voice. It had been twelve days since she'd last seen him, not that she was paying attention.

"Only if I get an invite from you. Wouldn't want the reputation of being an overbearing boss," he answered with objective diplomacy.

Gladys twittered and headed toward him. Laura noted the exaggerated sway of her hips. With a wide smile that they didn't see very often, Gladys closed the distance between herself and

Chase. "I'd think nothing of the kind. Always a pleasure." She actually batted her eyes at him.

"That's nice to hear." Chase returned Gladys's smile.

Laura gritted her teeth that a man could be so gullible. Didn't he see that Gladys had sized him up like a tasty morsel? If she licked those thin red lips one more time she would personally head over and pull out her tongue.

As for Chase, she would've figured that he had better taste.

Her student finished the post therapy stretch using exercise bands. She took the bands to the rear of the room to place them back in the inventory closet. A light touch on her shoulder startled her.

"Didn't mean to do that." Chase smiled down at her. "How are things going? Still enjoying the job?"

Laura nodded. Deciding that she was at a disadvantage stooping at the bottom of the closet, she rose. He didn't retreat and she ended up much too close for her own piece of mind. The closet door stood firmly at her back and she had no where to go.

"I've got a surprise."

Laura didn't respond. She didn't know how to respond. Chase seemed determined to start up a relationship. She had even more determination that any arrangement like that would never happen again. From the venomous looks that her boss threw at her, playing friends with the big boss would be disastrous to her tenure.

"I got tickets to see Wynton Marsallis."

"You're kidding." Laura grinned. Trust Chase to remember her hot buttons. What wouldn't she give to hear such a jazz legend? She sighed. "I can't."

"You can't, or won't?"

"Same difference." Suddenly she felt hemmed in by his presence, the offer, the expectation. It all felt like a thick woolen blanket on a humid day. She scooted out to the side for a chance to breathe.

"What's going on here?" Gladys asked from behind Chase.

Chase turned his head to the side, but didn't respond.

"Laura?" Gladys prompted.

"Chase…um, Mr. Westfield…knows that I like jazz."

"It's okay to call me Chase."

Laura wanted to slink away. She didn't know how to answer.

"Didn't know that you were friends." Gladys honed in on Laura.

"We aren't," Laura replied.

"At one time, we were." Chase didn't shift his eyes from her as he spoke.

"And that was a long time ago," Laura clarified. He looked as if he was about to respond, but thought better of it. Instead, he shook his head firmly. Couldn't he see that Gladys didn't want to hear about them?

"Are those the tickets?" Gladys boldly plucked the tickets from Chase's hand. She read the tickets, her eyes growing wide. Laura figured that she probably noted the value of the ticket and where the seats were located. "Never been to a jazz concert." Gladys's voice held lots of hope.

"Can't make it anyway. Have a dinner date." Laura had stepped out of the threat of such a mess.

Gladys looked up and smiled like a hungry shark. Meanwhile, Chase only stared down at her, no smile present. But Laura didn't plan to wait around and provide any more lies. With a quick excuse me, she skirted him and Gladys who'd actually inched closer until her shoulder brushed his upper arm. The sight of the woman fawning over Chase curled strings of jealousy in the pit of her stomach.

"Well I have to get back to work," Laura inserted into the silence.

Chase took the tickets out of Gladys's hand and held them out to Laura. "Maybe you and your date can use the tickets. I wasn't dying to go, but I thought you'd appreciate it."

Now Laura wished that she hadn't lied about having a date. Her main goal had been to let Chase know that she'd moved on. He couldn't know how lonely she was every night. He couldn't know what seeing him on her first day of work did to her. As much as she thought that she had gotten over him, seeing him in flesh and blood brought her feelings racing back at her as if by a sling shot. Every time she saw him or talked to him, she was close to defeat.

"Thanks, but I'm not sure that jazz is his thing." Laura supposed that her perfect man would be the ideal opposite to Chase, even if it was only in the imagination. "Well, the next student is due. Got to run." She greeted the student and led him to the curtained area across the room. By the time Laura finished treatment on him, the small group had dispersed.

Laura didn't know how Chase ended it with Gladys, but from her sudden departure and the rigid shoulders as she stormed out behind him, she surmised that Gladys didn't get an invite nor did she get the tickets.

"Wow, that was better than a $1.99 movie," Kasey whistled softly and then chuckled.

"Oh, be quiet," Laura scolded.

"Why didn't you take the tickets? I would've gone with you."

"No. I don't want anything from him."

Suddenly, the loud chatter of students filled the room. At least four athletes jostled each other through the door. Not only were they teammates on the track team, but they were also fraternity brothers. Their T-shirts were the first evidence of their fraternal Greek affiliation.

"Who's up first?" she questioned.

"That'd be me." One of the young men, acting like the leader, stepped forward. He squinted at her as if she was hard to read. "You're new."

"I've been here just shy of a month. Guess

you stayed healthy during that time. Didn't need our services."

"I'm Ned Parker."

Laura introduced herself.

"Oh, for Pete's sake, it's the college campus Casanova. Hey, watch out, Laura. He'll try to hypnotize you with those baby boy looks." Kasey remarked over her shoulder.

"I'm immune," Laura declared. He was a cutie, but all he did was remind her of her brother, Omar. The fraternity brand on his arm matched her brother's tattoo of the Theta sign.

"Don't listen to Kasey, Miss Laura."

"If you call me Miss Laura, I'm going to make your therapy sessions unbearable."

Ned nodded.

Laura questioned him about his injury, a pulled hamstring and sore Achilles heel. She recorded the details, noting that he had a small file with a recording of his injuries and treatment. The hamstring was a reoccurring injury. His tough training schedule for football and track took their toll on his young body.

During the assessment, Laura learned about Ned. Like any sophomore who had become an athlete, he had a healthy ego. Yet, his personality held a warm charm that she found appealing. Before long, he was confessing about the two different girls whom he currently dated and the pressures of keeping them separate.

"I'm glad that you're not getting into anything serious." Laura massaged his thigh, her fingers detecting the lump where the muscle tightened into a painful knot. "But, I must say that your method is a little on the dog side." She paused. "You know it's only a matter of time before they find out about each other."

"But I am serious about them. Both of them. I truly love them."

"See, I told you that men are up to no good." Kasey piped up from the other station.

"You couldn't fall in love with both women. Which one would break your heart if she left you?"

Ned's brow furrowed deeply. His eyes rolled up. Laura couldn't wait to hear what he came up with. His total self-absorption amused her. "I'd pick Fatima. Quiet. Smart. Gives me my space."

"Obviously she gives you too much space." Kasey and the other teammates laughed.

"Shh," Laura warned. If they kept up the noise, she wouldn't be surprised if Gladys came swooping in.

An hour later, the four members of the track team left. Their departure seemed to take all the life out of the room. The experience solidified what she liked about her new career. She'd made the right decision. What she did had a material benefit.

She mattered.

With the day at an end, she packed her bag and headed out.

"Hey, Laura, you want to get a drink at the Irish bar at the corners of Marsh Avenue and Stevenson Road?"

"Naw. I'm beat." Laura wished that she could say that she was going home to get ready for her date.

"Okay, but you know the uniform types will be at the bar. A man in a uniform wearing a gun is such a turn on." Kasey wiggled her hips.

"Too much information."

"I tell it like it is. There may be a couple of fine dudes that can stimulate your interest," Kasey teased.

"What about you?" Laura tried to shift the focus from her. "You have enough reason to restock your inventory."

"You're darn right. But I thought that I'd have a buddy."

"I've gone out with you to more bars in less than a month than I have ever done in my hometown. I need to recoup. By myself."

"Fine. I'll let you get your way—this time."

They parted company. Laura drove home, talking herself out of stopping at the grocery store for a few personal items. She'd manage on the tiny remnants of deodorant and low level of lotion. She'd have to go with ashy legs and hands that were dry and scratchy like sandpaper.

As she entered her apartment, the phone rang. She hurried over to the side table to answer it.

"Hey, Sis!"

"Omar?" Laura grinned, her mood immediately lightened. "Good to hear your voice. So what's up, little brother?" Laura knew better than to think Omar was calling for the fun of it.

"Have a proposition for you."

Laura pinched the bridge of her nose. Here it comes. Omar was about to ask her for money.

"You there, Laura?"

"Yeah." She wished that she could be firm with him. "Go ahead."

"Can I come over to tell you?"

She could pretend that she was too busy this evening.

"Do you have company?"

"No." Maybe she shouldn't have answered so quickly. Hopefully she didn't sound frustrated.

"Okay, I'll be right over."

"Don't hurry. I'm all tapped out," she said, wearily.

"I'm not borrowing money."

Laura didn't believe him. Guess she'd find out sooner or later what he was up to. She ended the call, trying to predict what her brother was up to.

Her stomach rumbled, pushing her to deal with dinner. She didn't feel like cooking a meal. Hopefully she had a few frozen dinners in the freezer. One look among the scant contents showed that she was out of luck. She had a tray of chicken breasts, but had forgotten to take it out of the freezer and thaw it in the fridge. She glanced at the pizza delivery number.

While a hot, cheesy pepperoni tantalized her,

guilt at the thought of eating such a thing made her hesitate. Maybe a shower would clear her mind and she could come up with something nutritious and filling.

She kicked off her shoes and pulled off her socks, tossing it toward the hamper making a perfect basket. Her victory dance needed some music. Seconds later the latest hip hop song blared over the speaker. She didn't get outrageous with the volume, figuring that her neighbors wouldn't appreciate her music listening experience.

The white overcoat was next as it landed on the back of the couch. Laura danced up and down the hallway as she unbuttoned her khaki pants. In the mirror she posed and shimmied her hips out of the pants until it fell to her ankles.

The doorbell sounded.

"Crap!" Laura pulled her blouse back down and hurriedly pulled up her pants. She forgotten to ask Omar how close he was. "Who is it?" she asked, approaching the door before leaning against it to look through the peep hole.

She gasped.

"It's me. Chase."

Laura clasped her hand over her mouth, just in

case he could hear her muffled scream. Why was he here? Better yet, how had he found her?

"I looked you up in the employee directory. I know that I should've asked if it was okay for me to come over, first. But I was also afraid that you'd say no."

"And no one could blame me for telling you to get off my doorstep." Laura opened the door enough for her body to block entry.

His gaze drizzled over her like heavy syrup, lingering over her hips, along her stomach and over her chest. Her traitorous body warmed under his attention. Laura gripped the doorknob for stability.

"May I come in?" Chase asked.

"Why?"

He smiled and then proffered a brown paper bag.

She stared at it, wondering, but not accepting it. Plus she wasn't sure that she liked the devilish smile he offered her.

"I know that you probably didn't have time to make dinner." He lifted the bag a little higher.

Laura sniffed the air, already determining that some sort of seafood made up the contents of the bag. Her favorite. He certainly played dirty. It didn't help that her stomach growled, long and low. She tried to cover it with a cough.

"Sounds like you shouldn't keep your body from eating."

"Fine. Take it through to the dining room." She gave way, gesturing toward the open dining area. What on earth was she doing? This man, had broken her heart and hadn't wanted a thing to do with her. Now he kept turning up with gifts. Not that she minded the visual that he presented. Following him into her apartment, she again admired the broad shoulders and toned body. His body moved with a powerful grace that was a mix between confidence and healthy ego. Traits that she found quite attractive, and appealed to her taste for the bad boy type of guy.

"Stop checking me out."

Laura almost stumbled over her dropped jaw. She'd been caught. But he didn't have to know. "You wish."

"All the time, babe." He stopped abruptly. "Dishes?"

Laura hurried past him to get the paper plates from the pantry. How embarrassing. She hadn't brought all of her plates from storage. Entertaining was far from her mind. Where the heck were the plastic forks? This wasn't fair. What must he be thinking?

"Hey, let me help you."

"I've got it." Her face burned as she pulled the sectional dinner plates out of the plastic bag. Then she set the knife and fork next to it with a paper napkin.

"You shouldn't be so stubborn. Let me set the table and put out the food, while you go do what you need to do."

"What exactly do you think that I have to do?" He was such a know it all. She placed her hands on her hips, waiting for his cocky reply.

"First things first, I think that you should pull up your zipper. Maybe after dinner, we can work on unzipping you."

Laura gasped, slapped his arm and ran into her bedroom. She promptly fixed her pants, mortified that she could've possibly thought he was admiring her. Instead, he was probably looking at her bright red cotton panties.

Chapter 5

Chase took a seat at the table. He was quite pleased with himself. As he glanced over the table, he figured that he should've brought some flowers. But he thought that looked so hokey. Right now he felt like the bull knocking over more than priceless china. So far, he hadn't been able to get Laura alone long enough to explain himself, talk about the past and propose the future in a clear manner. His emotional outpouring only seemed to scare her.

"The food is getting cold." He didn't want anything to ruin this dinner.

"I'm ready."

She had changed into a soft flowing dress that draped sexily along her hips, down her legs. He found the fluffy bedroom slippers endearing.

"Oh, sit." She shooed him down when he rose to pull out her chair. "You're making me uncomfortable with all this attention."

"I'll try to restrain myself." He didn't want to spook her. But it grew increasingly difficult not to reach out and trace the delicate shell of her ear, run his thumb along her bottom lip, hold her close to inhale her scent. Things that he used to do.

She took the spoon out of his hand, shooting a look of annoyance. "I'll serve the food."

He raised his hands in surrender and leaned back in the chair. How he wished that this domestic scene had a level of permanence. With that thought, hope was renewed.

"This is delicious," Laura exclaimed.

"It is quite good, isn't it?" He smiled as she sucked in the pasta, leaving a glossy sheen on her lips.

They made small talk as they made their way through the meal. They stayed with safe topics.

The upcoming daylight savings time actually earned a fifteen minute discussion.

"Chase, answer me this—why aren't you out on a Friday night basking under some woman's attention?"

"Those days are over. Not really in the limelight. No one is interested."

She frowned at him and then got up to clear the dishes. She moved around the table without speaking, yet he sensed that she had lots to say on the matter.

"What about you?" He wanted to turn the attention on her.

"Me?" She let out a loud laugh. Stopping in midstride with the take-out food containers. "I'm kind of focusing on me for the time being. A man would suck me dry."

"Ouch." He didn't dare ask who had turned her against his sex. He already knew the answer.

"What do you want from me, Chase Westfield?" She looked at him long and hard before storing the food in the refrigerator. "Is your conscience bothering you?"

He watched her set the coffee machine to brew a fresh batch. Her movements were deliberate and quiet, almost soft as she went to the cupboards to retrieve mugs.

"Yes, my conscience bothers me. It constantly jabs at my soul, calling me an idiot."

"You need to stop being nice to me. I'm not good at playing the bad guy," Laura responded, still tending to the coffee machine.

"Laura. Please listen to me. I didn't understand what you were going through with the loss of your mother. Your father leaving you and your siblings. And then my family turning their back on you for no reason."

"Everything was fine until our friendship turned into a complicated twosome. Can't even call it a relationship. You let your mother talk to me with contempt. Then, you turned your back on me because I wasn't good enough for you."

"That's not true, my love."

"Don't," she mouthed, no sound coming out of her mouth. She looked at him with eyes filled not only with tears, but also with pain. The raw emotion reflected on her face like a moon on a calm lake. His desire was to hold her in his arms. He moved around the counter to where she stood.

She stepped away from him. Her arms outstretched, warding him off. "Don't." This time her voice sounded small. "Let's not use the L-word. It's been overused in our case, wouldn't you say?"

He caught her wrist, immediately falling under the spell with the touch of her skin against his. She didn't pull away, but shook her head. Her eyes closed.

"Don't block me out." He pulled her against his chest. Her hands balled against his chest, but he didn't release his hold around her body. "Why can't you give me another chance?"

He touched her forehead with his lips. "We have too much in our past to give up on the future. We were childhood friends before we were lovers. Now, I want to be your soulmate." He felt her body shudder under his words.

She raised her face up to him. He could only hope that she had relented. That maybe she wanted to kiss him as much as he wanted to kiss her. Her lips parted but yet he waited.

"I'd say it's time for you to go." She pushed herself away from him.

Chase didn't expect such outright rejection. He certainly didn't expect the steady eyed, humorless

Laura standing in the doorway. Several words of protest came to mind, but he confidently shelved them away. Diplomacy didn't carry through to his limbs which had ceased any movement.

He walked out into the hallway, paused and turned around.

"You don't get it, do you?" Laura's voice sounded flat and hollow in the hallway. He didn't respond. There was nothing to say. It didn't matter what she said.

"I lived my life to please you. You were everything to me. I woke up thinking about you and went to bed, hoping that I had pleased you." She shook her head. "What a fool I'd been."

"Can we go back inside, please?" he whispered. His words stirred her anger.

She hesitated. But he didn't and walked back into the apartment.

"This won't take long," he assured. "You're not a fool. You've never been a fool. Yes, timing may have been off between us. But it never stopped me from caring about you."

"And that may be so. But you had an ego the size of Texas. You may have had ulterior motives for having me take this job, but I plan to use this opportunity to build on my experience before I head off elsewhere," Laura promised.

"Darn it, Laura. I can't believe that you feel nothing. There were too many good times between us. We made history."

She pursed her lips.

That was quite enough. He pulled her into his arms, his hands around her back. Without a seductive introduction, he planted his lips on hers. Lock and load. Her fists were balled against his chest, but her lips had softened under his pressure. He didn't relent, didn't pressure, simply maintained contact until he felt her hands open against his chest. A low moan, barely discernible escaped from her. His heart performed a crazy beat when her hands encircled his shoulders. She wanted him as much as he wanted her.

He knew it.

With that thought, he succumbed to the romantic thoughts that coursed through him. Her lips were warm and inviting and he plundered her mouth, laying claim to what she offered. His body responded aroused to the point that he felt as if he was a time bomb with a finite time before combustion.

His hands explored the length of her back,

seeking the warmth of her skin. He pulled up her blouse and slipped his hand under the material. Her smooth skin against his hands sent electric charges through his fingers and arms. He wanted his lips to follow suit and find bare flesh. His mouth eased away from her full lips and trailed a path from her jaw to her ear lobe and then her neck.

He trailed his tongue along the vein in her neck. She was so sweet. His hands discovered that she wasn't wearing a bra. Immediately he reacted. His hands slid along the sides of her body to the front and cupped her breasts, kneading and stroking his thumbs along the sides of the fleshy mounds.

He'd love to suck on each nipple. The thought drove him crazy. Pinning her hands over her head with one hand against the front door, he raised her shirt with his other hand until her breast was bared.

She emitted a soft moan.

And he wanted to hear her desire. Still maintaining his hold, he lightly brushed her nipple with his tongue. She pushed off from the wall, arching her back. He accepted her offer and covered her breast with his mouth. They were sliding down a slope where slowing down would be almost impossible.

"You play dirty," she gasped.

The air practically crackled with the heat of their shared passion. Chase didn't waste any opportunity to keep his lips fastened to some part of Laura's body. He'd missed touching her and having her body respond to him. Now he wanted to make up for lost time. Before his brain could break in with second thoughts or doubts, he lifted Laura and held her close to his chest.

He may not know where the bedroom was located, but figured going down the hallway would eventually get him there.

Her chest rose and fell in quick succession. His breathing grew labored, but not because he had walked down the hall into the master bedroom. That wasn't it at all. He wanted their breathing to mesh and work in rhythm. All he had to do was to look in her eyes and read the desire that had imprinted over her face. Gently he lowered her to the bed.

Laura unbuttoned his shirt, running her fingers along his chest, down his stomach. His muscles contracted against her sensual touch, making him suck in his breath. She giggled from her power.

"Don't think that you're in charge," Chase warned.

"And why not?" She brushed his nipple with her pinky finger, until he had to grab her hand to stop.

"This is my plan. I'm supposed to seduce you." He pulled her top over her head. Not that he needed any further stimulation for arousal. But the sight of her breasts and their chocolate dipped tips drew him. He gladly honored each breast with his attention. First, he blew on each nipple, as a precursor for what he had in store. Then he kissed each softly before covering them with his mouth. Totally unhurried, he sucked until the nipple puckered into a tight hardness that he then swirled with his tongue.

Her ecstatic gasps turned him on. He continued to play with her, sometimes dipping down to her navel. He wanted to melt away any of her inhibitions and join him on their sexual rediscovery of each other.

Her hands grabbed either side of his head as she groaned in pleasure. His hands gripped her hips. Her skin felt warm and firm. The pelvic thrusts begged for his attention. Again he honored what she didn't say, but what her body demanded.

"I want you, Laura."

She barely nodded. In her head she was battling against her rational side which was ready to condemn her. Her mind refused to succumb to her body's cravings.

He eased himself into her. Her warmth encircled him in a snug sheath. He found himself breathing through clenched teeth. Pressure in his head escalated as the tip nudged against the moist inner boundaries between her legs. She wrapped her legs around his hips, interlocking her ankles. He didn't mind, enjoying the close proximity.

They rocked to each other's beat. Nothing outside of their circle penetrated what they shared. Chase held on tightly to Laura, afraid that she would vanish within his arms. Their desire swirled with heated passion upward to an unreachable peak, building into a frenzied pace where he wasn't sure that he was still breathing. Was he even conscious? Her breasts rubbing against his chest told him that this was real. And then he felt her pulsate and he closed his eyes, clenched his teeth and held on for dear life as he joined her. Together they took the plunge, surrendered to desire and slowly made their way back to surface.

Chase laid his head on Laura's chest, listening to her heartbeat return to normal. The swell of her breast cushioned his head. Although he wanted to start their lovemaking all over again, he restrained himself. He knew that Laura would be thinking about what had just happened. He wasn't sure how she would react, so he simply rested.

The doorbell rang.

Laura froze. It took several seconds to force her mind from its fantasy with her and Chase to the current surroundings.

The doorbell rang again. This time, her visitor leaned on the bell a few seconds too long.

Laura looked at the clock. Then it came to her. Omar.

She pushed Chase's head aside and hopped up, looking for clothes that she could hurriedly wear.

"Guess, I'll get going." Chase reached for his clothes.

"Sure." Laura grabbed a dressing gown, but then thought better of that choice. Omar could probably look at them and know what they'd been up to. But to come to the front door with only a robe was like turning a floodlight on the situation. She grabbed her dress.

"I think we need to talk...eventually." Chase looked up from tying his shoes.

Laura shrugged. She wrung her hands as she hurried to the door. "Who is it?"

She heard a muffled voice with its familiar tone. "Omar, wait a sec." She looked through the peep hole and couldn't help smiling at her younger brother's look, always the smooth operator, sporting his hip-hop designer sweatshirt.

A glance over her shoulder showed Chase sticking his belt into the loop on the pants waist. She waited until he looked up and then placed her hand on the knob.

There was no time to bring closure to what they had just experienced. In his arms, she had been ready to accept whatever he wanted his world to be. Now on her own, with space between them, she had to face reality. Reality dictated that she realize that their time had passed and no future lay in a happy ending between them.

"Hey, little brother." They hugged before Omar stepped past her.

"Got any food?" Omar headed straight for the kitchen, his nose raised in the air.

"Leftovers." Laura joined him. Her eyes drifted over to her bedroom door. What was taking Chase so long? For heaven's sake, the longer it took for him to appear, the more blatant their action would be.

Omar nosed through the containers, rejecting the Lo Mein, but setting aside the Chicken fried rice and Schezuan chicken.

"Get a clean dish from the dishwasher." Laura called out as she headed down the hallway, leaving Omar busy with dinner preparation.

Laura opened the bedroom door and poked in her head. There was no sign of Chase. She opened the door and stepped in, glancing around the entire room. "Chase," she whispered. There was no response.

She stepped out of the room and headed to the bathroom. She knocked softly and pressed her ear to the door. The door opened and she almost fell in. "What's taking you so long?" she asked softly.

"I was wiping off your cologne. I'm heading to a meeting."

"And she might not appreciate the scent of another woman," Laura said, offering her two cents on the matter.

"Since you're fishing, I'll tell you," Chase replied.

Laura pretended to protest, but not hard enough to deter him from sharing the details.

"I have a meeting with my manager."

"Manager?"

"My contract isn't over, so technically he's still my manager."

"Still have jobs to complete?"

"Something like that," he provided.

Laura stepped back for him to exit. She wanted to ask more questions, but he looked ready to go and Omar was about to break what few dishes she had based on the sounds coming out of the kitchen.

"Omar, long time no see."

Good grief. She couldn't believe that Chase plunged right into things with her brother, hip-hop lingo and all. Although she certainly preferred Omar finding out than her older brother. Pierce would pitch a fit.

"Chase, what's up." They slapped palms and gave each other a one arm hug. "I see you're up in the crib."

"Yeah, man."

"I'm just passing through. Had to talk to your sis," Chase explained.

"Sure, man. Maybe I'll see you around."

"That-a be cool. You can save my bacon with your sister," Chase replied.

"No prob. Always got your back."

Laura hung back, leaning against the wall. She didn't want to see Chase to the door, knowing that he could take that opportunity to do something outrageous. Although a deep tongue kiss didn't seem like a bad thing.

After Chase left, Laura took a deep breath and faced the youngest Masterson. A knowing smirk crossed her face. She waited.

The microwave buzzed. Omar retrieved a steaming plate of chicken fried rice, grabbed a soda from the refrigerator and took a seat at the table. Laura slid into the seat opposite his, watching him shovel the hot meal into his mouth.

"Well, what do you want to know?" Laura broke her rule not to start the conversation. Unlike her eldest brother, Omar would take his time finding out the information. Unfortunately, her conscience prodded her.

"Can I move in with you?"

"Huh?"

"Planning to move back into the downtown area. Can't handle the cost of living on my own. Then I thought about you and it made sense."

"What about law school?"

"I may get a job at the university."

"But you're a high school teacher and coach."

"I'm no longer feeling fulfilled, so I started looking. Some of the jobs at the university don't require big degrees or a lifetime of work experience. I'm looking at various positions."

"Don't you have a girlfriend back in Hampton Mews?"

"Broke up. Hadn't planned on anything long-term."

Laura shook her head. His ex-girlfriend probably didn't know that it was a short-term commitment. Why the heck did these young girls lose their heads over her silly brother?

"It'll set Pierce's mind at ease if I stayed with you."

"Does he know that you aren't going to law school?"

Omar didn't answer, instead flopping down on the couch. He sighed heavily and leaned back his head.

"You know our big brother will be angry."

Omar closed his eyes.

"Talk to me, Omar. You'll have to face him, sooner or later." Laura walked around and sat next to him. They used to be close when they were growing up. Then once she went off to college, they hadn't reconnected. She'd always viewed him from her position as the big sister being inconvenienced by her younger brother. But now, feeling confused with her own state, she could understand the turmoil that he may be suffering.

"I got a job," Omar responded.

"What?"

"Starts at the beginning of spring break, but I've a lot of prep work to do. Officially, I begin in three weeks."

Laura sat up, poking him in the rib. "Spill it."

"I'm going to be a host for a television hourly spot featuring local artists, writers, actors. It's all about highlighting Atlanta and its celebrities."

"Omar, that's wonderful." She leaned over and hugged him.

"Teaching Physical Ed worked for me, after all. You know the singer, Stacy Watts? Well, she came to visit the school. We got to talking and she liked my voice."

"I suppose, among other things," Laura teased.

"She's not like that. Anyway, she gave me a number of a TV producer. The ball started rolling. Before I knew it I had an interview and audition."

Laura tried to pull back and really look at Omar. She wanted to see what all his girlfriends saw in him. He was a specimen of youth, especially with all the attention he gave to keeping his physique in tip-top shape.

"But I didn't get the job right away. They said they had narrowed the pool to thirty-five. Then a week later, they said it was down to fifteen. Then I went back in for a second interview. That time, I had auditioned under a test audience."

"You're kidding me. That would do me in." Laura made a face at the thought.

"I almost gave up. But I didn't want to have to admit to Stacy, if she ever found out, that I chickened out."

This Stacy person had a lot of pull with her brother.

"What do you think?" Omar pressed.

"I'm going to have to think about it." Not too many advantages seemed to be on *her* side. The biggest advantage for him was cheaper rent. She tried not to think about their many arguments when he left his basketball shoes in the living room. She didn't consider herself a neat freak, but she certainly wasn't on the same level of untidiness as Omar.

"I'll need to know soon." He stood and fixed his clothing. "Not to pressure you, but if I can't afford to stay in Atlanta, then I can't take the job."

"I know, Omar." She wasn't trying to be cruel, but nothing could be this easy. At home when Phillip gave Omar a hard time, she was the one to step up and defend him. But this was different. Even she had to cut the cord between her family and herself, once and for all. Though Omar may think of himself as a responsible adult, under her roof, she'd be worrying about him constantly.

Plus what happened if she wanted a little somethin' somethin', like earlier today. She was a grown woman and didn't want to feel as if she couldn't have a man in her house.

A man like Chase. Strong, handsome, physique of the gods, stamina beyond belief, with a wicked sensual rhythm that could generate a heat through her body with only mental recall.

"Sis?"

Laura looked at her brother's face. Good grief, he needed to stop with the puppy eyes. Life just wasn't fair. "Just for a bit. Get on your feet. Save some money. Then get out of my house."

"Deal!" He whooped it up in her apartment. Then headed for the door. "Be right back."

Laura chuckled. He was such a kid at heart. Heaven help the woman who could tame that one. She headed to her bedroom to change.

A few minutes later, she heard a steady thump that grew louder. Most of her living area was hardwood floor. And she could have sworn that she heard her furniture being dragged along the floor. Not only did she have to worry about the tenants under her, but what was that crazy, foolish boy doing to her polished floor. She hurriedly buttoned her shirt, slipped her feet into her bedroom slippers and marched down the hall.

"What the heck is that, Omar?"

"My stuff. I had it in the car. You know, just in

case you said yes." He had a trunk like the ones that freshmen students would drag out of their parents' minivan and haul into the dorm room.

"Look at what you're doing to my floor!" Laura was horrified to see several trails where the trunk had scraped off the polish on the floor. "Drop the trunk before I choke you."

He promptly dropped the trunk which sounded like a loud explosion.

Laura shook her head and stole a look at the clock to see whether the tenant below her apartment would come up now or later. She pushed up her sleeves and picked up one end of the trunk. "Let's go." She aimed for the second bedroom that doubled for a den in the small unit. She'd miss her little hideaway.

After the trunk and Omar were in the room, Laura escaped from the room. She stood in the hallway, shell-shocked. Having her brother as a roommate was never her intention. Seeing the massive quantity of his personal possessions left her slightly queasy that this was for the long haul.

"Hey, Sis." Omar poked his head out of the room. "I really appreciate what you're doing here. And I know it might feel crowded."

"Don't worry about it."

"Well, I don't want you to feel as if you can't have Chase over. And I might have a young lady over every now and again." He grinned sheepishly before ducking back into the room.

Laura's cheeks burned, more than a little embarrassed with the direction of his chat.

"So, when I hang this red sock on my door knob, it'll be my sign that I have someone. Let me know what you'll use." Omar stood in the doorway with a red sock hanging from his hand.

Laura never thought there was an actual thing as tongue-tied but all her words seemed to clog her throat. Discussing their schedule for sex seemed other worldly. As much as she thought of herself as being hip, she couldn't admit to this level.

"Here, I don't wear this pair anymore because of a hole in the toe." Omar tossed her a white sock.

Laura reached out and caught it. With her head down, she walked past him back to her room. "Thanks." She laid the sock on her dresser, took a seat at the foot of the bed and stared at it. Unfortunately, the symbol of her getting busy with a man only reminded her of Chase.

Chapter 6

"Achoo!"

"Bless you," Kasey responded. "For the third time."

"I think I'm going to have to call it a day after I finish this paperwork." Laura pulled a tissue from the box nearby and blew her nose. At first she'd thought that her allergies were acting up since the fall weather was so dry. Now with the achy muscles and headache pounding just below the surface, she had to admit that she was sick.

"You shouldn't have come in today. Now we're all going to be sick."

"Sorry for coming out of the house without my protective bubble. If I knew that my symptoms would have gotten worse, I wouldn't have come in." Laura glared at her friend. All she wanted to do was go home and crawl into bed.

"I can't afford to get sick. I met this really nice guy and I don't think he'll appreciate me rubbing my nose all over his beautiful face." Kasey wiggled her eyebrows. "If you know what I mean."

"Fine." Laura grabbed her paperwork and her briefcase. "I'll work at home. If I don't feel better by the morning, I'll call in."

"Cool." Kasey blew her a kiss.

It wasn't fair that the day should be this sunny and cloud free. Laura shielded her eyes as she emerged from the building. Her throat had gotten worse and she grimaced with each swallow. She pushed the button on her key chain to deactivate the car alarm system. Then she threw her briefcase into the next seat and turned the key in the ignition.

Nothing.

"This can't be happening."

She turned the key again. "What the heck!" Laura hit the steering wheel with her hand. Suddenly, her headache turned up several notches and now screamed its own tune in her head.

A car pulled up opposite hers at the curb. Laura placed her hand on the door handle. Maybe they could help. Otherwise she had to deal with a tow truck and the fee that went along with that service.

Raised voices caught her attention. She peered through her window to see what all the fuss was. If she wasn't mistaken, it was Ned and a young woman, probably one of his girlfriends. From the exaggerated facial expressions and the hands punctuating the air, she might be the ex-girlfriend.

Laura debated whether to pretend that she didn't see this obvious argument or tell them to take it elsewhere. Her runny nose and sweaty disposition didn't place her in a great mood. Either option stood the chance of her ill temper getting the better of her.

The door slammed and Ned stormed off, as much as he could with his hamstring injury. The girl at the wheel screamed Ned's name, but he didn't slow his pace. Then she tilted her head up and screamed. Now, that drew a few stares. It seemed as if the college crowd had become jaded souls. No one stopped to see if the girl was okay.

Laura pushed away from the car, which she used as support to view the drama. She tapped on the glass, startling the young lady. When the girl only stared at her, but didn't budge, she motioned for her to roll down her window.

"I'm not going to ask if you're okay, because I think the answer is pretty clear. But are you able to help me?" Laura asked.

The girl wiped her tears, sniffling in the process. She looked up at Laura. Her lips trembled, a sign that her emotions weren't really in check.

"I need a jump start." Laura pointed at her disabled car.

"I don't have cables," the other woman said.

"Shoot!" Laura stomped her foot in irritation.

"You're Ned's physical therapist, aren't you?" Laura nodded.

The girl frowned, shifting her view from Laura to the building.

"I'm not feeling well. So I left early. Kasey is handling my caseload today."

"I'm Fatima Henry. I'm done with my classes

for the day. I can give you a ride. Do you live around here?"

"Actually, not that far away. I'll direct you." Laura hurried over to her car, grabbed her briefcase and pocket book and headed to Fatima's car. She could feel the chills overtake her body. She had to concentrate to keep the dizziness that stood at the edge waiting for an inopportune time to descend. Fatima leaned over and opened the door.

"I really do appreciate this. I'm feeling awful and then to have the car break down is the capper."

Fatima pulled out of the parking lot. They headed to the west entrance to the campus. Laura provided directions, appreciating Fatima's knowledge of the area. She leaned her head back and closed her eyes. Her face felt as if someone was pressing down on the T-zone over her eyes and down her nose. Then her stomach grew queasy. She prayed for all green traffic lights.

"Guess you're wondering about me and Ned back there?"

Not particularly. Laura didn't have the energy to shake her head. Her eyes remained closed.

"Ned says it's over. I don't know why he takes things to the extreme." Fatima emitted a frustrated sigh. "He accused me of rushing him. We've been together for three years. I don't see why we shouldn't be engaged. But now that I'm calling him on his offer to be his wife, he can't deliver."

Laura heard a mournful sob. She opened one eye, hoping that her fear wouldn't be confirmed. But, oh no, Fatima had begun to cry. Laura sat up and ran a hand over her forehead to symbolically clear the headache and any fuzziness in her thinking. She couldn't have this girl crying while driving to her house.

"Fatima, why would you have a discussion about the ring and engagement in the car, and before the team plays?" Ned had made his decision. Or maybe Fatima made it for him.

"Yeah, but he's not playing. He's got another week of therapy, right? He's riding the bench."

"But it's still his team out there. He's probably frustrated that he can't get out on the field with them. Did you warm up to the subject? Or did you jump down his throat when he got in the car?"

"I told him that we had to talk. Plus, I know about the other girl. He kept trying to push me off. I learned from my mother that you don't let any man push you around. I say what is on my mind."

Laura felt like giving two snaps of her finger and a neck roll to go with that definitive statement.

"Don't get me wrong. I love him. But he can't be trippin'. Then he tried to break bad on me and told me that he needs to walk away and think."

Laura thought that Ned certainly had managed to make his young life complicated. Fatima, as much as she sounded tough, didn't have matching bravado in her heart. In their own way, these young people were in love. Who was she to judge?

"You really don't look good, Miss...I mean, Laura. You're sweating a lot. Do you want me to turn on the air-conditioning? Will that help?"

"Go ahead. Turn on the air." Laura swallowed. Her throat was so parched that she couldn't lick her lips, which were very dry. She closed her eyes for reprieve. The brightness made her headache worse. Her body didn't have any energy. Every action or body movement took great effort of mind and will to move.

The cool air blew into the car's interior. Immediately goose bumps raised on her arms. The chill seeped into her bones setting her teeth in a fierce chatter.

"I don't think the air is a good idea." After seeing her distress, Fatima pressed the button to stop the cold air.

Laura looked out at the neighborhood, thanking her luck that she was finally in familiar territory. The gated community of her apartment home complex raised her spirit somewhat. Situated in the downtown area, not far from another university hospital, the hub of city life didn't intrude in the residential calmness of the property. She'd tried to keep the conversation going, but definitely couldn't. All she could manage were directions. With a determined effort, she prepared herself to get out of the car, as soon as Fatima pulled in her reserved space.

"This is it?" Fatima peered through the windshield at the building number.

Laura nodded. Her stomach rocked, its queasiness hadn't left. She opened the door and almost tumbled out into the parking lot. Maybe she should have had Fatima take her to the emergency room.

"Here, let me help you." Fatima ran around the car to meet her.

Together, they stumbled their way up the path

into the building. Her preference for a higher floor now came back to bite her in the butt. She dreaded each step. She must remember to thank Fatima when she was feeling like her old self. The young girl had won points with her.

"Thanks, hon. I think I got it." Laura shook her hand at Fatima, halting any further progress now that the front door was opened. "I suggest you take a hot shower, take your vitamins and drink lots of liquid. You don't want what I'm suffering from." Laura paused to take a deep breath.

Fatima took the cue, looking more than a little worried. She ran down the stairs, only looking up when she got to the bottom. Laura gave a final wave and hurried inside. She barely made it to the bathroom before she upchucked.

In a full sweat, she dragged herself down the hallway. Her brother's door was open. She could tell that he was not in. She didn't pause. Her sights were set on her bed. Finally she touched the mattress with her knees and collapsed onto the bed.

Her throat ached. She didn't have any energy to make herself any sustenance. Her last taste was a mixture of toothpaste and mouthwash. Turning onto her side, she drew up her knees and moaned into the pillow tucked against her body. Where was an angel of mercy when you needed one?

Laura awoke with a start. The light had dimmed considerably. She squinted at the window and then at the clock. What time was it? A deep yawn overcame her. She stretched reaching her arms overhead. The sheet fell off her body.

Confused, she looked around, struggling to remember what was the last thing she did when she came into the bedroom. Her recollection may not be clear, but she did remember that she was lying close to the end of the mattress. At the very least, she was on top of the sheets.

She needed more light than the muted duskiness of the evening that made it through the mini blinds. She turned on the lamp near her. Stunned, she looked down at what she wore—one of her workout T-shirts. She raised the sheet and looked at her bare legs. Guess that was about it. Her hands immediately went to her breasts.

"I took that contraption off. Figured you'd thank me later." Chase stood in the doorway.

Laura forced herself to close her mouth. The soft snap of her jaw was the only sound in the room. Her hands still covered the soft roundness of her breasts. The bra and her clothes were stacked neatly on a winged chair.

"Bet you're hungry."

Laura followed Chase's approach into her room, looking disgustingly cheerful. He carried a tray laden with food. A white bowl had steam curling off its contents. Beside the bowl, a white coffee mug also had steam curling over the brim.

"Chicken noodle soup. Sorry, not from scratch. And peppermint tea." He sniffed the mug. "At least that's what I think it was. You had a few tea bags in a container, but no label. I can taste test it for you."

Laura shook her head. But that wasn't a good idea. Her head pounded from the sharp movement. She concentrated on pushing back the dull ache.

He settled the tray in front of her, whipping out a cloth napkin to tuck into her shirt.

"I think that I can do that myself." She snatched the napkin from him, clutching it to her chest. The last thing she needed was his fingers brushing against her skin. And certainly not in the chest area.

"As you wish. The soup is very hot." He hesitated.

"Thanks, but did you change me? My clothes are gone. Why would you do that?" she asked, a warm flush crept over her cheeks.

"You were so wet with sweat that you left an imprint on the sheets. I promise that I didn't linger."

"Liar!"

He grinned.

Her body blushed in response.

Chase stepped away as she ate. He desperately wanted to hover over her, but restrained himself. Watching her look miserable, he'd debated on whether to take her to the hospital. "I'll be in the living room. Holler if you need me."

"Where's Omar?"

He shrugged. "Didn't know that he was supposed to be here."

"He's living with me. Temporarily. I just thought that he was the one who let you in." She smacked her head. "Don't tell me I left the keys in the door?"

"Nothing like that." He couldn't gauge her to know whether she would understand. "I went to your job to talk to you. Kasey told me that you'd left early. Then, as I was leaving campus, I saw your car. That scared me, but I realized that I didn't have your cell phone number or any other number, except in your employee file. Luckily, I ran into Fatima. She was coming to talk to Ned. She told me that she'd left you looking like crap—her words." He opened his arms. "Here I am." He left out the details about how he had panicked and blew through several twenty-five-miles-per-hour residential zones to be there.

"I do appreciate it," she mumbled before closing her eyes. He retrieved the tray, allowing her time to rest.

Chase exited the room and headed for the living room. He took a seat, turned on the TV and settled back to look at his favorite sports channel. He was satisfied that she looked much better now. He heard the shower. Good. She was moving around. More than likely she had a case of the flu and it would have to run its course. He had taken her temperature which had been slightly raised. Tomorrow, he'd have to explain why he'd missed an important meeting with his boss and the university president.

Chase felt himself being shaken. He opened his eyes, momentarily disoriented.

Laura was looking down on him with a smile. "Oh man, what time is it?"

"It's seven. You dozed, but not long. I took my shower and then came out here because it was so quiet."

Chase rubbed his eyes. Remembering his role, he rose and headed to the bathroom. He found the thermometer. "I think it's time for a status check."

Laura took the thermometer and placed it under her armpit, depriving him of a second chance. They didn't talk. He listened to the beeps as the seconds ticked by. Finally the instrument emitted a chirp. He waited for Laura to hand it to him. "Still raised, but no higher than earlier today. I think you should take something for the fever."

"I will." She pulled a bottle of pills and shook out two in her palm. Then she threw them into her mouth and swallowed.

"Would you like a glass of water?" Chase

swallowed, imagining the pills being stuck in his throat.

"I'm fine." She grinned at him.

Every time she smiled or grinned, heck, every time she looked at him, he melted. Before he could rationalize his emotions he pulled her into his arms and laid her head against his chest. "I could just kiss you."

"What's stopping you?"

"Germs." That earned him a playful punch in his arm. "You're not a hundred percent. Let's not overdo it. We can catch a rerun of something before your favorite talent search show begins." He wanted to stay with her. Maybe he could keep her mind off sending him home.

"I'll return the favor one day," Laura promised.

"Anytime." He meant it.

She backed away from him. The attraction buzzed between them like a fast electric current, growing stronger with every second. In sickness and in health, they shared a connection. He didn't want to blink, feeling as if that would destroy the link between them.

"I'm ready to leave the bathroom," she indicated with her head bobbing toward the door.

"Sure." He didn't move until she raised his arm and ducked under to exit.

They spent the hour watching contestants dance their way through the auditions. Laura opted for another cup of mint tea. He ate a ham and cheese sandwich with a cold root beer.

"Now, that you said Omar is living here, where *is* your brother?"

Laura shrugged. "Omar has turned into a work fiend. He goes to his job and then volunteers at a local cable station."

"That's a shocker."

"Tell me about it. I'm wondering if it's the job or whether it's this girl that he's trying to impress."

"Then let me school a younger brother," Chase suggested.

"You?" Laura snorted. "I think it was always the other way around where you're concerned. Those girls would perform somersaults if they thought that they could get your attention."

"You were the only person I cared to impress." Now that she'd opened the door, he was going all the way. "I did it once and I'm prepared to do it again."

He watched her sip the tea. The TV show suddenly seemed too loud. Once and for all, he wanted to talk about this ugly swamp of distrust that lay between them. This time he wouldn't be deterred.

"Oh please, Chase, let's not start that again." Laura sighed and placed the mug down carefully. "Why pretend that this didn't end ugly? That you didn't walk away. That you didn't think that I was good enough for you. Money tends to bring out the real deal."

"I think we were both at fault. I can't deny everything, but I think it's unfair of you to make me bear the blame alone."

"And exactly what parts do you want to redistribute?" Her eyes narrowed. Her anger evident in the tight line of her lips. Even her shoulders froze in fury.

"I really hurt you." Talking about the past was like stepping into a minefield. Somehow he managed to get to a certain point and then had to bid a hasty retreat. But inevitably, a step in either direction created a blast. "All I can ask is if I can make it up to you."

"Chase, I don't want you to think that I can't forgive you. I do. I really do. But your constant presence in my life right now is making it painfully obvious that forgetting you is next to impossible. I don't want anything from you. Not because I hate you or anything like that. I have moved beyond you. It took a while, yes, but I did it."

Laura shook her head. "Now that I have my career in place, I plan to move on with my personal life. I don't want you to imagine that there is something between us when there isn't." She wiped away tears. "You have a special place in my heart, but it's time to put away childish things. We were young kids at heart, nothing more. We both believed in fairy tales. I know we have this crazy attraction, but I think that it's because we know this all must end." The tears flowed as she rose from the sofa and headed into her room.

Chase listened to her blow her nose. He'd heard everything she said and understood everything that she didn't say. Words didn't matter at a time like this. Maybe it was his arrogance that made him believe that he could sweet talk her into falling in love again.

One thing was sure, he wouldn't give up on what he knew existed—even if Laura had.

They had become friends before they became

lovers. They had bared their fears and inspirations with each other. No one could ever replace what they meant to each other. He agreed that their youth had been a factor. But he was a grown man and he knew what his heart, soul and body needed.

Enough pleading for her to take him back. She'd matured. Now she was a woman who had experienced a heartbreak with the first man in her life. He knew from his friends who had dogged their women about the lasting bitterness and anger they caused. All their relationships, thereafter, would be measured against that experience. He now witnessed the harder edge to Laura's perception. Unless someone walked in her shoes, they couldn't hold her decisions against her.

The fact didn't stop him from his goal. He wanted Laura as his best friend, lover and eventually as his wife. Instead of taking the direct route to reclaim her heart, he needed to regroup for a change in strategy. He wouldn't quite declare that a war was in progress. But he had to rely on gut instinct and stamina to outlast her protest. Winning her trust would be a long, hard journey. The competitor in him was ready.

"Chase, you don't have to babysit me." She had resumed her place on the sofa.

"You're right. I think you're on the road to recovery." He scooted to the end of the chair. "You have my number, if you need me." He stood, took his dishes to the kitchen, made a big production of cleaning up whatever mess he made, then retrieved his keys. "Take the day off. I'll let Gladys know." He headed to the door, opened it and walked out.

As he walked toward the stairs, a wide grin spread across his face. Laura had been shocked to see him easily accept her suggestion. She hadn't recovered quick enough to tell him goodbye.

The key would be to keep her off balance until her head caught up with her heart that she still loved him. He was in such a good mood that he whistled in the parking lot as he headed to his car. He managed to share greetings with passersby. It was certainly a brand new day for him at nine-thirty at night.

At work, Chase had settled into his groove. His morning found him in one meeting or another. The afternoons were spent on the track. His team of assistant coaches led training. Occasionally, he stepped out on the track to share his tips. Regardless of his occupation, the track held a special place in his heart. Sprinting was an addiction that lay deep in his bones.

"Time!" He looked down at the stop watch, then at the athlete bent over to his knees trying to catch his breath. "Straighten up so the air can get into your diaphragm. Ned, what are you doing? Your starting position and timing is off. You're running slow enough that your grandmother could pass you on her Sunday drive to church. I need you to come to practice focused." He placed an arm around Ned's shoulders. "Listen to me, you are my star athlete. But don't take it for granted that it allows you any perks."

"Yes, coach. I don't know what happened. I think I got distracted. You know, my mind…"

"See, that's what I'm talking about. On the field, nothing else matters. Any problems you're having off the field stays there. When you crouch in that position at the start line you turn your focus on the end. Each step should be strategically placed and succinctly timed to make the win happen. You'll have men next to you, breathing down your tail and probably in front of you. But it's not over until you get to the finish line and break that tape. You feel me?"

"Yes, sir."

Chase gave him a reassuring pat on his shoulders. "Go do starting drills with Coach Haskill." Ned dully trotted over to the assistant coach. The young man had the makings for greatness. Maybe that's what Chase's coach had seen in him long ago. He'd shown his frustration to Ned because he took his natural talent for granted.

But was he doing the same with his personal situation?

An hour later after practice, Chase still remained on the field, walking the lane. In the past, his every step for an upcoming race would play in his mind. He knew how precise the motion had to be. Nothing entered his head between him and a race. Once he'd mastered the technique, he couldn't shut it off.

Sitting in the grass, he slowly stretched his hamstrings and calves. Then he stood and finished stretching the quads and Achilles heel. Almost by rote, he performed some of the drills that his coach always made him do.

His joints ached, protesting a little too loud for

comfort. He sucked it up. In lane four, he lowered his frame into the starter position. He kicked out each leg and repositioned them. Then he fixed each hand behind the line. His routine before getting ready was the same. If he deviated, he lost badly. Superstitious or not, he didn't believe in messing with a sure thing. Then he lowered his head, thought about the goal at hand and then raised his head. All he waited for at this moment was the sound of the pistol.

The millisecond after it sounded in his head, he shot out of his stance and aimed for the center line within his lane. He pumped his arms, urging his legs to move, sucking air through his teeth.

Chase Westfield, Olympic Runner. By the time he got to the end of his race with himself he felt like an utter failure.

He limped off the field, hoping that he'd make it to the bleacher before he collapsed. Pain like a hot tipped fork jabbed at his knee in one leg and through his ankle and foot in the other. By the time he got to the bleacher, his limp grew more pronounced. He gritted his teeth, cursing himself for testing his ability, but more so, for revealing his weaknesses. Finally he pulled himself to a seat in the front row.

He lay back with the leg that hurt more raised on the seat.

"You know if you stay here any longer, the grounds crew may think that you are a life size wax figure."

"Stop gloating and help me." Chase looked up into Laura's amused expression. "How much did you see?"

"I'll keep that to myself to save your dignity." She sat on the bleacher near his foot. She rested her hand on his foot.

"You used to massage my legs," Chase prompted.

"Hmm."

He wiggled his leg for emphasis. "Please." He'd whine for her killer massages any day.

"I'll oblige." She raised his leg and scooted closer. Then she gently warmed the muscles, worked out the tension and soreness with firm smooth strokes.

Chase gritted his teeth even harder. The pain cut through him to the bone. But the key to a quick recovery was to keep the muscles and joints moving.

"I thought that you were out of town."

"Nope. There's too much here that the president wants to see done before year end. Haven't traveled since I started here. Were you looking for me?" Chase hated to sound so hopeful.

"Kind of."

"How can I help?" She needed him. "Do you need something?"

"It's not for me, personally. I wanted to talk about Ned."

"Ned?" Chase raised himself onto his elbows. "Something happened?" He knew that he'd been hard on him at practice. He swung himself into a seated position.

"He's okay. Well, not really or else why would I be talking about him? I think that he's pushing himself too hard before his body is ready. And I'm worried about the number of recorded injuries."

"I had a lot of injuries. This isn't your after-school community team sport. This is life."

"Chase, listen. I know what you're saying. But you need to look at my report."

"Haven't seen any," he admitted. He expected his assistant coaches to monitor the active team members and those who had been sidelined for whatever reason. Obviously someone had dropped the ball and it was hitting him squarely at his feet. "What does it say?"

"I think that he'll need surgery before he blows out his knee. There isn't enough ice and heat treatment for the persistent swelling. I know that he's in more pain than he's letting on."

"Is that why he's been so distracted? My fear is that he'll cause injury because his mind isn't there."

"Could be." Laura sighed. "I do know that he's having a hard time with his girlfriend, Fatima."

"Good grief, would these women just back up and leave my team alone? It's like they see dollar signs whenever an athlete starts making a name for himself. Next thing you know she'll be looking for him to sue for child support." He slapped his knee, full of frustration.

He stared out at the field, the overhead lights already burned bright. Another day gone. What was he doing with his life? Was he even helping these guys achieve their dreams. Realizing that Laura hadn't responded, he turned to look at her.

Her expression met his questioning one with a cold, hard unsmiling fury. She didn't blink. Her mouth twitched, but he knew better than to think it was because she was about to smile or cry.

"What did I say?" But he already knew. And it was too late to retract. "I'm sorry." Great. It sounded more like a question, as if probing her to see if that was enough to get on her good side.

"Ned isn't the victim. He can't have both worlds because it's obvious he can't handle either one. Even if Fatima initiated the contact, and I very much doubt it with lover boy, he didn't have to respond. And since you're so concerned about his daddy status, maybe you should incorporate abstinence or have them get a pack of condoms after their practice drills. Then they wouldn't have to face the financial burden of their creation."

"Ned has so much potential." Chase drew in a ragged breath. "Enough with that. Tell me more about Ned's physical condition. Are you telling me to pull him from the active roster?" Chase gritted his teeth.

"That's your call. I was simply bringing it to your attention. I don't want to see him chewed up and spat out when the system is done with him." Laura kicked at a pebble.

"I'm his coach and I'm his friend. I was once in his place, hoping that my body wouldn't be tray and fail me. While he's under my care, his mind, body and soul are my responsibility."

Chase didn't mean to lecture Laura, but the topic sometimes got the better of him.

Laura tapped her foot, a clear sign of her irritation. "Is this your self-diagnosis of what went rong on your end?"

"I hope that you don't think I was talking about us." He wasn't going to side step what he knew ran through her mind. "We're only talking about Ned."

"You brought up your team and athletes at large, Mr. Spokesman. Tigers don't usually change their spots, so you tell me."

"Tigers have stripes." He grinned, but dropped the smile when her eyes narrowed at him.

"Fine."

Chase watched her walk down the bleachers.

"You know, Chase, I wasn't your enemy," Laura tossed over her shoulder.

They were at odds. But this was a minor setback. He wasn't dissuaded from his goal. He retied the lace on his running shoe to run, or limp, after her.

"Would you come to my Halloween party?" He'd never thrown a costume party. The thought popped into his head and he went with it.

"What? Aren't you a little old for that stuff?"

"Oh, you're on a roll tonight with the jabs. But, I'll allow you your barbs if you accept my invitation. I have a broomstick if you need it for your costume." He smirked.

He saw her dig into her pocket book, take out something and throw it at him. The small missile landed short on the bleacher. He looked down to see the red and white mint candy still in its wrapper, not the worse for the ill-fated pitch.

He reached down, retrieved it and popped it into his mouth with a toothy grin. "Thanks." He followed her retreating back toward the gymnasium. It didn't take much effort to catch up to her, despite her attempts to lengthen her strides. "Are you coming? Or, are you scared?" he taunted. "Afraid that you won't be able to abstain from me?" That one got her right between the shoulder blades when they twitched.

She got to the door first. Silhouetted in the doorway, the shadows partially hid her face, but hugged the outline of her toned body. She had no idea of the effect. He wasn't about to tell her. He slowed his pace, not wanting to make her run to keep the distance between them.

"Hanging around these kids must have done something to your brain. You want to have juvenile costume parties for some odd reason. I'll show up, but you come near me, say anything to me, even breathe on me and I'm going home. I'd rather be watching a rerun on UPN than talk to you." She slammed the door shut as he reached for the handle.

He chuckled.

Chapter 7

"Laura, are you going to the costume party?" Kasey asked. Half her body disappeared into Laura's refrigerator.

"And what are you looking for?"

"I didn't eat breakfast. Thought you might have had something yummy. You got too much cottage cheese and yogurt." She wrinkled her nose at Laura who entered the kitchen. "Are you on some health food kick?" She sized her up. "It's working, but I'm not sure the cost outweighs the results. You don't even have any darn waffles." Kasey slammed the freezer door closed. "A girl could pass out from hunger in this place." She peeked down the hall. "Where's your sexy brother?" She pushed up her breasts and licked her lips. "If I was a few years younger, the things I would do to him."

"Out! I'm ready. Let's go." Laura ushered Kasey out the door. All she needed was for Omar to hear Kasey's declaration and he would come sauntering out in something obscene. The boy was such a player, but then so was Kasey who had rebounded from Ray with catlike ease.

They made their way down the stairs noisily with the shoes clacking and their conversation raised over the heels clip-clopping down the stairs. Laura's car still chose to be temperamental. Luckily she had been able to catch Kasey before she left for work. Her loud chatter was okay in the office to keep the mood lifted, but early in the morning, she simply wanted to strangle her.

Kasey pressed the remote to disengage the locks. From her vantage point, Laura saw the fast food wrappers of meals long gone. Mail was strewn on the seat and floor. And there were clothes. Just her luck that she had to see Kasey's collection of thongs sitting on top of the My Booty Pleasure shopping bag.

"Come on. We're going to be late as it is," Kasey urged.

Laura eased into the car and gingerly moved the bag and its contents over. Kasey took the hint, grabbing them and tossing them into the back seat.

"Shouldn't those be in your home, maybe in the underwear drawer."

"Hadn't decided whether I like them. While I'm driving, I look at them and touch them," Kasey explained, rubbing her fingers together for emphasis.

"As long as you don't say that you try them on in the car." Laura shuddered to think of the possibilities given Kasey's indiscretions at times.

"That's a thought." Kasey started the car and left Laura's neighborhood with a squeal of tires, an impatient honk of her horn and a rude hand gesture to someone who didn't yield to the four-way Stop sign.

"By the time you're done, I won't be able to show my face in my neighborhood again," Laura sighed.

"Don't worry about it, hon. Need to stop for coffee?"

"Didn't you say we're going to be late?"

"Guess you're right. Gladys will have a sour look on her face, like she sucked on a dozen limes, if we're late again." Kasey weaved through the morning traffic, heading into the downtown Atlanta area. "You know you didn't answer me about the party."

"Was hoping that you'd forgotten." Laura usually didn't react to taunts. It hadn't worked with her brothers and sister. Why at her age did she react to Chase's silly remarks? "I changed my mind."

"You can't. I want to go, but meeting all those celebrities makes me nervous. I need a buddy."

"What celebrities? This is a Halloween party."

"But Chase is big name. I'm sure he's got friends on the Who's Who list. Can you just imagine? Maybe I'd nab myself a fit, handsome somebody with bank." Kasey smacked her lips as if she could taste the wealth.

"You sound evil. And too much like what Chase was accusing Fatima of doing to Ned." Laura had told Kasey all about her last ill-fated talk with Chase.

Kasey pulled into the faculty parking lot. "Promise me that you'll go. I know that Gladys will be going. You don't want her to put her meat hooks into him."

Laura wrinkled her nose. Gladys wasn't much older. But she let the staff of women know that she was man shopping. This type of discussion didn't bother Laura, except when Chase's name popped up on a list of eligible men on campus. She wanted to take her black pen and mark out his name with an NA—not available.

Laura and Kasey walked into the physical therapy area. The other employees already at work had solemn expressions. No one quite met their eyes. Laura wanted to inquire if everything was okay but decided against it when she saw her boss emerge from her office. Gladys motioned for them to enter. They were only fifteen minutes late, albeit for the third day in a row.

Laura looked over at Kasey who bit her lip nervously. They didn't have time to exchange any last minute words for their story about being late. Guess she'd have to wing it.

"Sit down, ladies. Let me get to the point. We

had an emergency meeting this morning." Gladys remained standing with folded arms.

"Sorry we're late. My car wasn't working. Kasey came to give me a ride." Laura decided to jump in with an excuse to avoid one of Gladys's lectures.

Her boss waved away her explanations. "The budget process for the following year begins by next month. One of the things that we have been instructed to do is provide excruciating detail on our department, structure and treatment methods and costs. What type of equipment we're using. Everything that we do or touch."

"That's a pain. You're talking about long hours to get that together," Kasey complained.

"Glad you see the point right away. The reason for this exercise is that the university may be out-sourcing this area."

"Do you think they've already made up their minds?" Laura asked.

Her boss finally sat behind her desk. She looked miserable, as if she had already turned over the possibilities. She sighed, shaking her head, but said nothing.

"Let us know what you want us to start on," Laura prompted. She'd never seen her boss look defeated and she felt a stab of sympathy. "Guess there will be lots of late nights."

Laura went back to work, still stunned by the latest bad news. She looked over to Kasey and for once, the young woman was quiet. Everyone was lost in their own thoughts.

Too new to have made many ties, Laura didn't have quite the same concerns. Instead, she dreaded having to find another job with little experience. She'd hoped to strengthen her skills before moving on to private practice.

Leaving the campus meant leaving Chase. Was that such a bad thing? Maybe destiny had made a decision for her, to move on. The question would be if she should stay in Atlanta, or make a clean break.

Somehow she felt as if she were running away. From whom—she understood. But why? She didn't have a clue.

Laura settled down for the long list of clients she'd postponed until after their department meeting. She made her apologies but didn't go into specifics about the overhaul that could be underway. No word had spread regarding how many departments would be affected.

Today, instead of the track or basketball team pouring into the center, the day belonged to the gymnastics and lacrosse team. Laura grabbed her pad in preparation for her interview with the new patient. The gymnast was emotional, with tears welling as she wondered if she'd heal quickly. Laura understood the fear because of the severity of the muscle strain in her lower back. Laura duly recorded her range of motion, strength and how well she could ambulate. As expected, the gymnast's pain threshold sat at the highest end at a ten.

After the girl had undressed and donned a robe, Laura had her lie on her stomach. Using gel and deep heat, she warmed up the area. Because of her sensitivity to pain, she only used soft tissue technique on her. To help her patient to relax, they talked about her courses, family, her pet rabbit, what she planned do after college.

After twenty minutes of manipulating the muscle, Laura used two cold compresses on the area to reduce the inflammation. She left her on the table for the remaining ten minutes.

There was no time to catch her breath. Already, it was time for the next patient. Before long, the morning flew by.

Lunch didn't prove to be any better. Instead of her full hour break, she had to take a shortened thirty minute one, and Kasey disappeared without a word. Laura opted to find a quiet spot at the student union building. She ordered a pulled chicken BBQ sandwich and milkshake, then found a table in the far corner. For the next hour she planned to read the latest bestselling novel that she'd picked up from the neighborhood bookstore.

"Hi, Laura," a shy, familiar voice interrupted.

"Fatima?" Laura reluctantly placed her finger between the pages. The story had just taken an interesting turn. "How are you?" she asked politely.

"Do you mind if I join you?" Fatima's question came out hesitantly. "I wanted to talk to you."

"Have a seat." Laura placed her bookmark in between the pages and snapped it shut. "You've got my attention."

"I'm going to a *doctor's* appointment." Fatima still had her gaze fixed on her hands.

"Nothing too serious, I hope," Laura offered, when Fatima failed to continue.

"I might be pregnant." Fatima leaned forward.

"I took a test yesterday. You know, I was late," she mumbled, her discomfort evident. "It showed up positive." Now her eyes filled with tears. "I'm so scared. I made the appointment, but I'm afraid to go." She wiped her nose, suddenly looking like a teen about to face the grim realities of life. "Will you go with me?"

Laura inhaled sharply. Today wasn't a good day for major drama. Yet she hated to disappoint Fatima. Heaven help her if the test results came back positive. Then the consequences had to be considered.

She shoved the thought back. No need to rush too far ahead.

"The doctor's not far away. It'll probably take an hour."

"Since it's your first visit it might take longer. I wish I could go with you, but I can't. Does the potential father know?" Laura knew that she was prying. But Fatima had opened the door and invited her in.

Fatima looked away toward the throng of students looking for an empty table. "I haven't told him. It's Ned." Her tears rolled down her cheek. Large luminous eyes stared back at Laura.

"Go to your appointment. Get that done and over with. If your home test results were a false positive, then you don't have to make any sudden changes."

Laura put her hand on Fatima's arm. "But regardless of the outcome, you need to do some thinking. This isn't a solo act. You and Ned need to talk about lots of things." Laura didn't embrace her role as counselor with open arms. However, leaving Fatima to deal with this on her own seemed heartless.

"Yes." Fatima accepted the tissue that Laura gave her. She wiped away her tears and stood. "I'm not as scared as I was earlier." The young woman walked around and hugged Laura with unexpected fierceness. "Thank you for being there."

Laura stared at the exit where Fatima left. She wished that she could go with her to the doctor. Was she a bad person for hoping that her results were wrong? Could Ned handle the responsibility? Or a better question, *would* he? Chase's mocking voice came to her with its ominous foreshadowing.

The afternoon only had one return patient. Otherwise Laura spent the remaining hours writing up reports and calling doctors' offices. She couldn't wait for it to be over.

"Hey, you've been quiet. Don't let this morning's news hit you too badly. We went through the same thing two years ago. I think it's only to make the board of regents happy and to show them that we are being serious and fiscally responsible." Kasey had popped in after her extended lunch hour in a bubbly mood.

"Maybe, but Gladys looked quite shaken up," Laura countered.

"She's a Nervous Nelly."

"Or, she knows more than she's saying," Laura replied, feeling it necessary to read all the signs.

"Never thought of that."

Halloween came rolling in before Laura had mentally prepared herself for the big party event. Many staff members buzzed about details they'd heard. The invitation list did promise quite a few celebrity sightings. The amount of publicity this party got only made her more nervous.

Chase had made himself scarce, leaving her to wonder if he truly meant to invite her. She saw him at the all-department meetings but he barely spoke to her. Once he did come over to the office but then he was in Gladys's office for most of the visit. Even Kasey asked her if they'd fought.

She could use attending the party as a way to see what he'd been up to. But that could be tricky since she was the one who'd told him not to come near her.

One afternoon, she'd headed to the track for some quiet time before she had to tackle files for the looming, all-important report. She'd spied Chase performing his drills next to his athletes. Gone was the suit, replaced by sweat pants and tank top. She couldn't tell if he was racing at his original strength, but she could size up his body as one hundred percent phenomenal.

Once, he looked over in the direction where she stood but she melted into the shadows. After a brief moment, he returned to his task. It didn't take long to see his strength return. The marked limp that he suffered after running his drills had been reduced to a slight one.

How long would he be contained with his administrative job when his body returned to its former state? The thought scared her, holding her back from entertaining any happy ending with him. She'd survived and moved on under the same conditions. A repeat performance didn't appeal to her.

"Are you going to sit there all night and stare at the wall?" Omar danced in her bedroom doorway. His favorite singer, Beyonce, belted out another top hit over the radio.

Laura smiled. She had drifted for a few minutes. One glance at the costume set out on the bed and her stomach did flip flops. Why was she taking fashion tips from Kasey? Her costume was an all black, skin tight, faux leather outfit. She was supposed to be a female super hero that kicked butt in a sexy get-up.

In the store, the costume looked reasonably decent. Across her bed, the top looked too small, too tight, too short. The pants would have required her to starve herself for a week. She'd even bought a thong for the occasion, considering that the sleek material would showcase any unsightly panty lines.

"If you hurry, I'll drive us there," Omar offered. "My man Chase extended an invite to me, too."

"What's the rush? The party starts at nine. We don't have to be there to greet the other party goers." Actually, she wanted to enter when the party was in full swing and lights dimmed.

"That's true—I don't want to be the first one. Have you ever been to his place?" Omar asked.

"Once."

"Good, then you can tell me how to get there." He ran into his room and emerged with a turban on his head. "What do you think?"

"Genie?" His frown told her that she was way off. "Maharaja?" His mouth opened to protest. "Give me a hint."

"I'm a sultan. I have a harem."

"When does the harem show up?" she teased.

"They should get there by 9:15 p.m. I have three girls in their harem girl outfits who will follow me around all night."

"How the heck do you get three girls to agree to do something so stupid?" She'd been kidding about the harem. Her brother was so outrageous.

"I lay down the charm. Give them my smile and voila, they fall into a swoon."

"The trouble with that is that you believe it."

"'Cause it's true, Sis. You've got exactly fifteen minutes."

Laura closed her bedroom door and turned to

face the costume one more time. The outfit would draw lots of attention. But only one person's attention mattered. He'd been ignoring her long enough. "Let's see how strong you really are," she murmured to herself.

First, she had to put on her makeup. If she was going to vamp it up then her face had to be its best.

"Ten minutes," Omar announced outsideher room.

Laura took a deep breath and refocused. She pulled out her makeup case, the size of a small carry-on luggage. The entire line of cleansing treatment, foundation, concealers and colors probably totaled over five hundred dollars. Her secret addiction had always been a contentious matter when she was growing up. Applying her makeup took no time. She had too many years of practice when she snuck on her makeup at school and then wiped it off before coming home.

"Five minutes."

"Shut up, Omar. You're making me nervous." With her face in place, she decided to work on her hair. The super hero she imitated in the comic book wore her hair in a tight ponytail, which she replicated with holding gel. She snapped the ponytail holder in place, turning in each direction to check the views.

Since her costume was two pieces, she was dressed in no time. She held out her hands to the side, looking at her under arms. They could do with some tightening. Once she pulled up her arms, the tank top pulled up a little showing her skin. She wrinkled her nose. Thank goodness the color was black. Maybe to everyone else she would look slim. From where she stood she had other opinions.

The black faux leather pants hugged. She ran her hands down the length of her legs. "Okay, Laura, you can do this." She'd have to do a self pep talk all the way to the Chase's.

"Let's go. Hurry up. Can't miss the timing of my harem girls. Or else I'll have to depend on you and that ain't happening."

Laura swung open her door to give him a piece of her mind.

"What did you do to my sis?" Omar stepped past her, looking around the room. "Laura!"

She punched him in his arm. Good. She'd passed sibling evaluation. It was time to hit the party.

* * *

Either people were eager to be at Chase's party or being fashionably late was no longer en vogue. There was no parking on the street. They had to find a spot on a side road one block away. Thankfully she wore boots instead of the stilettos that Kasey had insisted the outfit needed. Who would kick the bad guy's butt in three inch heels?

As they approached the double doors, Laura slipped behind Omar. The small group standing outside the front door didn't budge or pause in their conversation. Maybe she would be unnoticed. Omar opened the door. Laura put a restraining hand on his shoulder.

"Even if it is a party, maybe we should knock.

Omar ignored her. "Come on. Let's see if Chase is around."

That proved to be difficult. Most of the men were in costume. She didn't know what he'd wear.

"See ya, Sis. No need for you to chaperone." Omar pecked her on the cheek and disappeared into the crowd.

Laura felt momentarily lost. She was a big girl, though. She walked through the living room, looking for any familiar face at this point. Music blared and many groups were involved in loud, animated conversations. She had only been at the university for a few months, and didn't have the courage to simply walk up and join in.

Spying other guests outside on the patio, she went outside hoping that she'd run into Kasey. Knowing her friend, she probably wouldn't show for another hour. Maybe she could call her and tell her to hurry up.

"You look like you're about to take flight," a muffled male voice said into her ear.

Laura turned, expecting to see Chase grinning at her. And maybe it was him but she couldn't really tell in the ninja outfit, along with full head covering.

"What's your name, sweetheart? You're killing in that outfit—the whole dominatrix look."

"If you really want to know, calling me sweetheart isn't the way." Chase would pretend to be another guest to mess with her. She didn't think he'd opt to sound like a loser.

"You're one of those uppity ones. Beg your pardon, Miss Missy." He bowed, but didn't stick around for her to continue. Didn't take him long to latch on to another single female, more than likely using the same lame line.

Laura headed to the bar. A glass of wine would settle her. A few appreciative whistles followed her on her way to the bar. The bartender had his back to her as he fixed a drink. She slipped onto an available stool and turned to look out at the modest outdoor crowd.

"Laura, are you loving it?" Kasey waved madly from the other side of the yard. She broke away from a group and headed toward her in a blood red flamenco dress.

"I'm about to order a glass of wine. Want to join me?"

"Sure. How do you like my Carmen Jones outfit? Even found a wig like the one Dorothy Dandridge wore."

"Just like her twin sister." Laura laughed.

"Whatever. Look at you. You are working that outfit, Girl. You must have had the guys panting after you when you passed them."

"They barely looked up from their drinks."

"What about Chase? Can't imagine that he let you walk past him."

"I wouldn't know. One bozo came up to me, but I don't think that was Chase. Doesn't matter to me if he sees me or not. I'm not pressed."

"Don't lie to me. I saw you scanning the crowd."

"Only to thank him for inviting me to the party."

"I bet you want to thank him, all right. You must be wearing the push up bra I suggested. Haven't ever seen so much cleavage on you."

"The top is small." Laura pulled at the neckline

"The top is the right size, but now you finally look like you've got some boobs like a real woman." Kasey leaned back to admire.

"How much have you had to drink? You're getting less classy by the minute."

"Say what you like, you know I'm not lying. Hey bartender, don't you agree. Look at her. Doesn't she appeal to your senses as a man?" Kasey hopped off the bar stool and stood with her hands open, presenting Laura as an exhibit.

If the floor could open but a crack, it would be enough for her to slide into it. Laura's cheeks burned, humiliated by her friend's drunken display. And then to make her the object of her stupid comments.

"Well, are you going to ignore a customer?" A loud hiccup popped out of Kasey.

The bartender put down his towel and turned toward them. Chase hadn't hired help for the occasion. Instead, he stood at the bar in a bartender costume, looking at her and Kasey.

"I can offer you a club soda with lime," he said pointedly to Kasey. Without waiting for her approval, he fixed the drink with lots of ice and set it in front of her. She scowled but took the drink. "I can take a hint. I'll go find a better bunch of party goers than you."

"You think she'll make it to the other side of the yard without spilling the drink?" Laura gazed after her friend.

"She'll be fine. I do have a few hidden helpers for folks who drink too much. And I have a list of taxis that have been alerted that they may have a couple fares tonight."

"How thoughtful."

"You underestimate me. Let me fix you a drink."

"Nothing too strong."

"Light. Fruity. Hmmm. Let me think." He busied himself behind the bar. Laura watched him pour a little of this and whole lot of that into a shaker with ice. After a few firm shakes, he poured the chilled contents into a martini glass. He slid it across the bar to her. "Try this."

It was pink like a Cosmopolitan, but he did a few more things to it than was in a standard Cosmo recipe. She raised the glass to her lips and took a dainty sip.

The fruity flavor hit her hard. Sweet and smooth like a berry flavor, then as her tongue warmed the liquid the sharp taste of underlying alcohol filled her mouth and nose.

"Good, but definitely only one for me tonight." Laura didn't have a problem knowing her limit.

"If you find that you can't drive home I do have an extra bedroom."

"I'm sure with all these pretty young ladies dying for your attention that that room is already reserved."

"You have a vivid, if erroneous, imagination. On the first count, there is no lady falling to the ground on my behalf. As you saw, no one came over to this bar. But look at the Greek Adonis bartender over there. See how the women of all races, socioeconomics and shapes flock to his bar. But you'll hear no complaints from me. You're the only one that was drawn to me."

"Don't flatter yourself. Your back was to me."

"I'm not buying that explanation. Even in a crowded room we would find each other, despite your hasty threats last time we talked."

She sipped her drink, mainly to keep herself from losing her senses as he talked. She held out the glass, visually examining its contents and the glass. Maybe he had inhaled its fumes and now it messed with his mind.

He leaned over and slid his hand along her hair. "What the heck? Feels like your hair is frozen."

"It's the gel."

"I wanted to run my fingers over your hair."

"Who knew that this ten dollar gel could keep your hands out of my hair?"

"Fine. But nothing you have can stop me from kissing you. I want to taste your incredibly sexy lips. I love the outfit by the way. Sexy is an understatement. You got Halle beat."

"Lucky me," she mocked.

Chase groaned and leaned over to kiss her. Laura considered hesitating but only for a blink of an eye. She couldn't resist if she wanted to. She opened her mouth under his single minded action. His tongue swept her mouth. He kissed her lips softly sucking her top lip, then her bottom. If she didn't have to balance herself on the bar, she'd have grabbed his face to engage in full lip lock. She'd settle for his kisses, intermittent nibbling and tongue sweeping across her lips.

Instead, she got Kasey pulling her arm. "Laura, oh my g—" Kasey interrupted. "Sorry. But it's really important!"

Laura pulled back from Chase. They held each other's gaze until Kasey popped into their peripherals.

"I just got a call on my cell phone. There's been an accident on campus involving three cars and the police."

"Do you know anyone in the accident?" Chase hadn't taken his eyes off Laura.

"Yes." Kasey sobbed into her hands. "It's Ned."

Chapter 8

Omar remained at the party. Laura, on the other hand, accepted Chase's invitation to go with him to the hospital. Kasey, at the last minute, decided to tag along. What little Kasey knew, she shared. The information sat heavy and cold in Laura's stomach.

"I can't believe that he was running from the police." Chase shook his head. His face was a grim mask. The playful sexy banter between them was long forgotten. "Do they think he was driving under the influence?" He banged the steering wheel.

"That's a possibility," Kasey responded from the back of the car.

Laura wished that her friend wouldn't answer Chase's questions. He was basically working out the scenarios in his head. Although he threw out the questions, he didn't relish hearing the realities. She placed a comforting hand on his arm. It wouldn't do for him to barge into the hospital with blind anger.

"Has anyone notified his parents?" Laura asked a question she determined as safe.

"Don't know. I would assume so. My information came from one of the paramedics who called me because he thought that I lived near the campus."

Once at the hospital, they ran into the emergency waiting area. Not only did they make enough noise to cause the entire lobby to look up at their entry, but they must have looked a sight. Laura could see the questions and then an understanding dismissal given the time of year as they looked at her all black get up, Chase's bartender costume, along with apron and Kasey's Carmen Jones, whose wig was slightly askew.

Chase took the lead and headed to the registration desk. The lady looked at them warily but asked them to wait a moment. She got on the phone and shared their request to see or get news about Ned. She nodded, tightened her lips and then set down the phone.

"Ned's parents are in there now. His father will come out to talk to you. You may have a seat."

They walked over to the seated area, but they didn't want to split up where the vacant seats were located. Instead they moved near an empty area where the soda machines and other snack machines were kept. No one spoke to the other. Then a distinguished man walked toward them.

"Mr. Westfield? I'm Ned's father, Frank."

"Nice to meet you. These are my colleagues," Chase introduced them, clearly impatient to get to the heart of the matter.

Frank Parker didn't appear to hear anything Chase said. "Ned's in surgery. They're not sure how long it will take since there is extensive damage to his chest and legs." His jaw tightened. He coughed and ended with clearing his throat. Though no tears formed, his dark, chiseled face reflected the torture of a father not in control of his son's well being.

Kasey sobbed into her hands. Laura pulled her into an embrace.

"What happened?" Chase asked.

"Apparently there were two cars drag racing, both drivers were under the influence. The cops chased them, setting up road blocks in the process. Meanwhile, Ned drove into the intersection unknowingly and got sandwiched between them. When the cars spotted the cops they tried to do some stunt driver maneuvers and lost control. Apparently the pile up was bad enough that they thought everyone had died."

"Did anyone?"

"One passenger who wasn't buckled in…died.

"How tragic," Laura murmured.

"Tragic. Those SOBs have one of our students on the brink of death," Kasey's voice raised.

Chase shook his head. Laura nodded, taking the cue.

"Kasey, let's get some air. I have to call Fatima anyway."

"Who's she?" Ned's father asked.

"His girlfriend," Chase answered.

"Oh, I've never met any of Ned's friends. I often wondered if he was adjusting well to school since he didn't talk about it. He did talk a lot about you, Coach. He looks up to you."

Laura held Kasey in her arms with a grip that didn't allow for any arguments. Outdoors the air had turned chilly. Not the time for a tank top. Hopefully, Kasey could pull herself together because it would be a long night.

"I'm sorry. You're probably wondering why I'm blubbering," Kasey said.

"Not at all. It's been a horrendous shock to all of us. I can't begin to think of Ned not recovering or pulling through the surgery. He's a good kid." Laura meant it.

"Reminds me of my little brother."

"Really. Looks like him?" Laura realized that as much time that they had spent together, Kasey didn't talk much about her personal life.

"Looks a little like him, but he really acts or rather acted like him. He's gone. It's been two years but I still miss him so much." Kasey broke down again. Laura debated whether Kasey needed to be in the hospital in her current state of emotion. Yet she sensed a serious fight on her hands if she suggested that Kasey should go home. Kasey wiped her eyes using her dress.

"Zack went to the prom with his date in a limo I paid for. I figured it would be a great gift from his big sister. The car was a stretch limo that three other couples shared with him. He looked so grown up. It hurt a little to think that my brother was about to be his own man in a few years."

Laura pulled out some paper napkins she had stuffed in her bag from a fast food restaurant. The paper was harsh, but it was better than nothing. She offered it to Kasey.

"After the prom, instead of heading home with the limo, he sent the driver away. I'd arranged that the driver would take them on a ride through Atlanta before heading to each of their homes." Kasey took a shuddering breath.

"Didn't the driver try to get word to you? I know that it's not his responsibility, but still?" Laura asked.

The company did call me an hour after it all transpired. Too late. Zack didn't answer his phone. Later they said that they'd all gone to a friend's house whose parents were out of town. They'd gotten drunk and then decided to go joy riding with the father's convertible. Some were sitting on the back of the car, if you can imagine. Zack drove. His friend sat in the front with his girl-friend sitting across his lap. The result wasn't pretty. The two who managed to survive the crash said that Zack had drank more than half a bottle of vodka by himself. Zack was probably the same body weight as Ned."

"My heavens." Kasey's vivid portrayal rocked Laura. A chill crept through her system at the imagined carnage. All she could offer was a shoulder for Kasey to cry on. Some of life's lessons were so hard to live with. "Maybe we should go to the chapel."

Kasey nodded. Laura led her back into the hospital. She received directions from the hospital staff. "You go ahead. Let me talk to Chase for a second." Kasey nodded and headed for the elevator.

"Everything okay?" Chase looked at the elevators closing.

"Her brother died in an awful drinking and driving accident. The memories are too much. I sent her to the chapel. Any word?"

"Nothing. If you want to take the car and take Kasey home, here are my keys. I'm going to stay here."

Laura took the keys. She wasn't sure if Kasey

had the stamina to wait it out. "I'll take her home and then come back."

"No need. I can get a cab."

"I want to."

He paused. "Sure." He pulled her into his arms. They hugged tightly in the middle of the emergency waiting area. Laura closed her eyes, gaining strength from the safety of his embrace. "I'm glad that you were there with me when the news came. And now you're here."

"That's what friends do."

He kissed her forehead. "Well, thank you very much, my friend."

Laura smiled. She saw the tiredness etched around his eyes. Before she caved and said something stupid, she placed her hand on his chest. "I'll be back."

Laura took a shower, mainly to refresh herself and chase away any sleepiness. Dressed in more practical clothes, she was better prepared to stay in an unforgiving chair for hours. She packed a sandwich, a couple of apples and an oatmeal bar with a bottle of water into a lunch bag. Chase had to be tired of the vending machine by now.

After filling Omar in on the latest developments, she jumped back into Chase's car and headed for the hospital. At first she didn't see him, but he'd managed to find a darkened area. The poor man would wake up with a stiff neck because of the unnatural way he propped his head as he dozed. Laura slid into the chair next to him careful not bump him. She glanced around the room for Ned's father, but he must have returned to the surgery area. His mother obviously didn't want to leave his bedside.

Chase stirred. "How long have you been back?" He stretched and yawned.

"Not long. I brought you a bit of sustenance."

He took the bag, his enthusiasm for better food clearly evident. He pulled out the sandwich.

"It's turkey and Swiss. Hope you like it," Laura said.

"This is fine. Thank you."

Laura enjoyed watching him eat. Between mouthfuls, he winked at her, showing his appreciation. She had never seen someone demolish an apple in a few bites. Maybe she should have packed double helpings.

An hour later, Ned's father approached them. Laura checked his face for any sign of a smile or lifting of spirits. Instead, he looked as grave and solemn as he did when they first spoke. She interlocked her hand with Chase's, bracing herself for the news.

"Ned is a strong boy." His father's voice wavered. He cleared his throat. "He'll need youth and that discipline you preached to get him through this. He may have to get additional surgery, but they were able to stop the bleeding. One of his lungs had collapsed." Laura didn't know the man, but she understood pain. She led him over to the chair. "His legs…they look like something from another planet with the amounts of screws and contraptions on it. His career is over." Ned's father looked at Chase. "There is no way that he will be able to run again. They're not holding much hope on him being able to walk."

"No one should count him out." Chase walked away from the group and stared toward the doorway that acted as a gateway to hope, joy and tragedy. "Mr. Parker, I don't care if you have to lie to that boy, even if he's unconscious, you tell him that you expect to see him running again. There will be time for life's cruel streak—a time when the crowds no longer care."

Laura stepped up and touched him under the elbow. Chase meant well, but his fervor was lost on Ned's father who appeared to have accepted the doctor's prognosis.

"We're not going to give up hope. We have to be strong for Ned." Laura held his hands, looking into his eyes.

"Mr. Parker, Ned has a family of friends and staff here on campus. Please let him know that he is in our thoughts and hearts," Chase said.

"Thank you. He's in ICU, of course. I'm going to check in at a hotel in the area."

"You are welcome to stay at my house," Chase offered. "Could get costly."

"I know. But what does it all matter if there is a change and I'm not nearby. Wouldn't be able to live with myself." Tears welled in his aged face. The grief covered his entire body, which seemed to double over under the weight.

"Is he conscious?" Laura dared to ask.

"He opened his eyes, but didn't look anywhere except straight ahead. The nurse told me to talk to him anyway, maybe he can hear even if he can't communicate."

"Well, take that as a sign that he will recover and

fight through the pain to be the same loveable Ned."

No one spoke. Laura figured that they were each sending their small prayers for Ned's recovery.

Chase drove Laura home. They sat in the car parked in front of her apartment building. The entire day had taken on a surreal quality that left him feeling as if he was drifting in and out of a nightmare. He hadn't checked on his home or the party since he left. Hopefully the revelers hadn't behaved too badly to upset the neighbors. Mundane concerns like that seemed so shallow when there was a young man fighting for his life.

"I think you should get some sleep. Tomorrow is another day for waiting and watching. At least we don't have to deal with going to work, or not."

"I don't feel like sleeping. I'm exhausted, but I don't want to close my eyes." He turned to look at Laura, frustrated that he couldn't explain any clearer.

"Seems wrong to be able to get in our comfortable beds and fall asleep."

"Exactly. It's a freak accident. And to say it

shouldn't have happened to him sounds crass because it shouldn't happen to anyone." Chase banged the steering wheel, his frustration already at full capacity.

"Well, I'm going to say good night and head in. Call me tomorrow and I'll go with you." She leaned over and kissed him softly on the cheek.

"Don't go."

Laura had her hand on the door.

Chase didn't want her to open the door. He didn't want to play games and figure out how to penetrate her defenses. No sweet talk to woo her to stay. His emotions had tanked at Ned's status.

"What are you asking of me?" She didn't remove her hand from the door, but she listened to him.

"Don't want to be alone."

Laura sighed. "Is that all you want of me? To keep you warm."

"I'm not trying to offend you, Laura. I simply need you." He didn't say anything further, he'd run out of things to say.

"Let me pack a bag and I'll be right back."

Ned's condition hit him hard on several levels. The teams would be rattled that the outside world affected one of their own. Being used to hearing about various sports related injuries were part of the career choice. But this—this challenged their image of invincibility.

On a personal level, Ned's condition and being yanked prematurely from the sport sent Chase into déjà vu. Although he didn't have the same devastating, physical issues, he could understand the overwhelming fears that Ned would face. It was the most lonely state.

Now he had to rally the remainder of the team to focus on their individual goals. He wanted to tell them that youth could flit away in the blink of an eye. That they should live their lives with no regret, because the real do-over in life—unlike sports—doesn't work.

"See, that didn't take long." Laura flopped into the seat next to Chase. She smelled like strawberries and her demeanor had considerably lightened since they sat in the parking lot.

"Did you eat an entire bottle of strawberry jam?" Chase inquired.

"Silly, I used a new body spray from my favorite toiletries store."

"You smell like the pastries my grandmother

baked when I was child. Sometimes she used strawberry jam. Ever since, the scent reminds me of her." He snapped his fingers. "I must remember to call her."

"That makes a girl feel good that she reminds a guy of his grandmother."

"You know I didn't mean it that way." He grinned. He started the engine and pulled out of the parking lot. With the streets deserted in the early hours of Sunday, Chase made it home in no time. His house and lawn were littered with remnants of the party.

"I can see that cleaning up will have to be a priority. You're certainly bringing down the property value," Laura said.

"Why do you think I brought you here?" He exited the car before her punch could land.

They walked past the trash strewn lawn and headed toward the side gate. Chase opened the door and entered his back yard. "Looks like the neat ones were contained back here." He looked around the various furniture and decorations for any wayward trash. There wasn't any. "Feel like a dip in the pool?"

"Are you crazy? What will I do with my hair?"

He shrugged, totally at a loss for women's fears. "I thought all you had to do was wash it."

"Wash, deep condition because of the chlorine, blow dry, hot curl."

"Sounds like an awfully long process that seems a bit unnecessary."

"Be quiet. Go swim, suck water, shrivel like a prune. I will sit on the lounge chair and babysit you."

"Sounds like a plan. What if I lifted you, like so?" He scooped her up, enjoying the shock on her face. "And walked over to the pool." She shrieked and struggled in his arms. "Then dropped you into the pool, like so."

"Stop, Chase. You play too much." She tightened her grip around his throat, cutting off his air. "Please put me down."

Chase set her down and watched her gingerly maneuver her way from the pool's edge. Not until she was safely away sitting on a lounge chair did she look at him with total irritation.

Chase turned back to face the pool. Laura sat at his side. All this bravado about making her his soulmate didn't overshadow the ever-present doubt that he could ever win back her affection to the level that it once was. The fact that Laura would spend the night, although in different rooms, stirred his hope.

Tonight of all nights after coming back from the hospital, he treasured her willingness to set aside her reservations. He recognised that heavy, dark burden now adding weight to his emotions. The spiral downward occured whenever he thought about the young man and the unfairness of life. His anger over the situation mixed with his residual frustration over his own circumstances spread through him like a virus tensing his body like a fighter ready for a match.

He wanted to roar, *bring it on!*

Instead, he went for the next best thing and plunged into the rippling water with no desire to be graceful. He pushed through the water, staying submerged, gliding along the tiled surface toward the opposite wall. His lungs protested, but he ignored the call for air until he was in arms-length of the side before exploding to the surface.

"Isn't that water too cold?" Laura called from her seat.

"Freezing." Chase grinned. The water was the perfect temperature to give him the jolt he needed to work the tension from his body. "If you joined me, you wouldn't feel so left out."

"Not on your life, *Boss*."

"Ouch. Yes, I am technically your boss. Like the way that rolls off my tongue." He grinned. He wasn't ready to come out of the pool. It was more than flirting with Laura. He could do that on dry land. His muscles needed that workout that he used to commit to on a daily basis.

"Since I don't want to be around when you get out of the pool, I'm going indoors. When you decide to stop playing your adolescent games, you know where to find me." Laura turned and walked inside.

"Gosh, you have a beautiful backside." He pushed off the side with his feet and propelled himself midway before turning his head to breathe. The freestyle was always his favorite and he enjoyed the long reach of his limbs as he glided through the water. What would have happened if he had pursued swimming? He'd been good at both sports and maybe he could have pursued both, but his track coaches wanted all or nothing. In those days, only a few athletes had managed to convince their coaches that they would play two sports. Times had changed.

He rounded his third lap. No regrets. He carried that motto through to everything in his life. Constantly looking over his shoulder and acknowledging the doubts would have sabotaged any strides he made.

Yet he did have one regret. She waited in his house, maybe entertaining her own doubts about why she was there. He had invited her over to be near her. But now he greedily wanted more than that. What could he offer in return? She wouldn't believe him anyway if he was to say anything meaningful to her.

He pulled himself out of the pool. In the outdoor cabinet he had extra towels. He grabbed two and wrapped his waist with one. With the other he vigorously wiped his head and arms. Most of the water pooled at his feet.

The house was quiet. Maybe she'd fallen asleep. He walked to his bedroom. Still no sign of her. His other two bedrooms were at the opposite side of the house. He headed over there, first looking in the room that doubled as his office. The next room, which he furnished with a full-sized bed and dresser, was also empty. Then he heard the shower.

Good, she hadn't run off scared out of her wits.

Satisfied, he went to his room and also took a shower. Again his brain gave in to wishful thinking. Would they ever share a shower, among other things, as husband and wife? He had to turn off the faucet and wipe his face to see if the thought disappeared.

The key to a successful athlete was one who listened to his body. But there was no advice to take if the body didn't know what it was talking about.

He sat on the edge of his bed staring at this closed door. How did one go from being the number one enemy to asking for her hand in marriage? The problem was that he didn't know how to proceed. But he did know that he was committed to that outcome.

Laura put on her oversized T-shirt, looking down at her bare legs. Thank goodness she had shaved them.

As she climbed into bed, she knew that she wasn't fooling herself with what she would really rather be doing. Chase had given her the invite she wanted in more ways than she could remember.

What was she so afraid of? Losing her heart? Not likely, since she'd lost it years ago. Since reclaiming it, she didn't have to worry about being a lovesick pup. She'd vowed never to leave her heart out in the open to be trampled or neglected again.

She could enjoy this turn in their relationship without any emotional commitments. They both didn't want anything further from each other—on that she was sure. All they could offer each other was friendship. Anything further was asking for trouble.

No man should have the responsibility of making her feel complete. Yet, she didn't need anyone to confirm that she and Chase shared something so special that it could only happen once in a lifetime.

She spritzed another dose of strawberry delight on her arms and legs, with a quick spat on her hair. Before she could lose her courage, she walked through the living room and headed for his great white bedroom door.

She knocked on the door, nervous at her boldness. He'd bared himself, shocking her speechless. Now it was her turn and the planets didn't have to be in special alignment for this sighting.

When he responded, she swung open the door. He sat on the edge of the bed as if he knew she'd come. She hesitated. Did he sense the steamy fantasies about him that she entertained?

"Did you need an extra blanket? Pillow?"

She shook her head at each offer.

"Are you hungry?"

She nodded, walking forward toward the bed.

"I can fix you anything you'd like," his voice deepened.

She reached him and slid herself between his legs. With one swift motion she pulled off her T-shirt and tossed it on the bed.

"Soup? Salad?"

She pushed him back onto the bed.

"What can I do for you?"

"Make love to me."

Chapter 9

Laura wanted to block out the events of the evening. She knew that pushing it to the background didn't change the results. But for a couple of hours she wanted to sink into oblivion and let her body release the controls of her thoughts.

Looking into Chase's eyes, allowing their gentle darkness to skim over her body, raised her temperature. He pulled her closer, laying his forehead against her stomach. She stroked his head, playing with the wavy grade of his hair.

"Do you really want to do this? I want you so

badly. And I don't want you to hate me for any of this."

She raised his chin with her finger. "I can't hate you." She straddled him on the bed, resting on his lap. "There will be time for talking. Later." She lowered her mouth to his, seeking the warm attention of his lips.

His mouth welcomed her with an intoxicating invite that made her hunger for more. His tongue touched in a sensual dance, courting her for a willing response. She wanted all of him. Their lazy rhythm rose to the moans rumbling deep in his throat. The vibrations drove her senses wild. With his face sandwiched between her hands, she matched his pace until she pulled away for a much needed breath of air.

"Did you bring in water?" Chase gasped.

She shook her head. Her head tossed back as her chest rose and fell. "What's with the water break? I hope your stamina is the only thing that's not working," she challenged.

"I'm not a gambling man, but here's a quarter that you'll be asking for water before I do." He pulled out a quarter from his wallet lying on the bed and tossed it onto bedside table. "Ready," he taunted.

Laura felt as if she was about to jump onto a roller coaster with its unexpected dips and frenzied turns at a titillating speed. Her adrenaline hovered, waiting for her signal to spike. She matched the wicked glint he tossed her way. "Set," she countered.

He lifted her off his lap and moved her to the side. She watched him undress with deliberation. She almost giggled madly when he retrieved a hanger and proceeded to hang his robe. Then he turned toward the bed and posed in all his naked glory like an athlete in the Ancient Greek Olympics. "Go," he shouted.

He dove on the bed. Laura couldn't contain herself and shrieked, her excitement uncontained. She scrambled toward the head of the bed. He crawled up toward her and pulled her down between his legs.

Laura didn't want to feel the cool air between their bodies. She pulled him down, wrapping her legs around him to keep him in place. He was aroused, nestled between her sexual folds that grew moist merely thinking of him.

"You play with the bottom half. I play with the top," he gasped. First he rocked his body, rubbing his chest against her breasts whose peaks were insanely sensitive. The hairs on his chest provided enough friction to make them harden into a tight pucker.

Her legs opened, unlocking him, for the moment. She arched, giving him the go-ahead to attend to her breasts before she screamed. His hand played and stroked one breast, while his mouth covered the other. Each pull made her stomach tingle from sheer pleasure. Her fingers worked his back from soft to deep tissue massage, reacting to the yearning between her legs.

She couldn't take it anymore.

Gripping his butt, she worked her way down to his arousal. Raising her hips she rubbed herself along his length, nudging him that she was ready. He ignored her, still content to play with her breasts. She wiggled her hips while rubbing the thick muscular pads of his buttocks. Did he want her to beg?

A moan escaped from her lips. Too late. He heard her plea. A devilish grin slowly spread. Then he actually chuckled. She gritted her teeth. She could be as competitive as the star athlete was. Before he could react, she slipped out from under him and slipped onto his back. Now it was her turn.

She sat on one buttock, letting her moist lips tantalize his neck. She heard him giggle in the pillow and leaned forward to whisper in his ear. "Give up?"

He tried to pull her off, but she was firmly planted.

"Play nice and I'll let you turn over. Otherwise I'm going to stay right here."

He settled down, then turned.

She invited him in, providing her own natural, moist refuge. His face tightened and his hands gripped her hips, trying to hold her still. But she didn't want to be still. She moved her hips over him, rocking back and forth in slow rhythm, feeding the inner hunger. They rode the dips and the high points, pushing further out to the limits.

She held on to his shoulders as an anchor. Instinct told her that they were fast approaching a precipice. She couldn't stop even if he wanted to. But she was ready to take that leap and hang on for the unknown. Her soft grunt, mixed with his guttural moans, escalated to a frenzied pitch.

They took the leap together, hip to hip, locked

in pure, natural ecstasy. Their bodies pulsed with the climactic throb as their organs talked to each other. Laura waited for their bodies to stop, not wanting to rush the aftereffects.

Besides, rushing the conclusion would hasten the fact that she desperately needed a glass of ice cold water.

The following morning, Laura finished scrambling eggs. She had already put out the toast and apricot preserves, thinly sliced turkey sausage and a few strips of bacon, upon Chase's insistence. The eggs provided the finishing touches to the breakfast.

"Do I smell coffee?" Chase looked like he had pulled an all nighter. Dark circles sat under his eyes.

"You're not only having coffee." Laura scoop eggs onto his plate.

"Don't worry, I'm famished. Didn't sleep well after...we—"

"I noticed that you tossed and turned a lot." She sat at the place setting next to his. Where to begin the conversation? She passed him the other food items. He wasn't really looking at her.

"I'm going to the hospital this morning," Chase stated.

Laura couldn't tell whether his tone meant that he wanted company or not.

"I'm not doing anything this morning," she offered.

"I can take you home."

"Oh." She picked at the bacon, breaking it apart. "Chase, why the sudden change in you?"

"What do you mean?" He sipped his coffee. The food remained untouched, getting cold. "It's morning. It's time to get on with our lives."

"Basically the sex is done, so no need to dilly-dally."

"I've got a lot on my mind. Ned is important to me."

"I agree. But you aren't Ned and Ned isn't you. You can't shut out the world or put it on hold until things are neat and tidy."

"Great advice coming from you." His eyebrows shot up in mock surprise.

Laura stamped down her rise to defend. "Let's call a truce. I don't want to fight with you. We don't have to think or talk about the future. Let's take it one day at a time."

"Sure." He drained his cup and excused himself.

Laura looked at the breakfast, irritated at the wasted effort she had put in to fix the meal. While clearing away the dishes, she felt as if they had stepped back in time. When he'd been a runner, he'd wanted his career to get to the perfect point before he could think about anything else. He closed himself off to his family—and to her. His mother blamed her for the self-imposed exile. But then again, his mother had blamed her for worse.

Her cell phone chirped. She frowned in the direction of the noise, wondering who the caller was. Omar knew she had left with Chase. No more bad news, please. Retrieving the phone, she answered. "Fatima?"

"Laura, I got your number from Kasey."

"Hey, slow down." Laura grew alarmed over the urgency in her voice. "Are you all right? Where are you?"

"I'm outside the hospital, but I can't go in. I don't think that I can handle seeing him all smashed up. What if he dies? I couldn't stand it if he dies. I wouldn't have him. I don't have his baby."

"Fatima, did you drive there?" The girl did not need to be alone.

"Yeah," she sobbed.

"Stay there. Sit in the car, play some soft music. I will be right over." Laura rushed to the room and started packing. "Fatima, do you hear me?"

"Yes, I'll stay here. But I don't know for how long. What if he dies?"

Laura didn't want to hear about Ned dying. The possibility existed, but there was no need to keep drumming it into everyone's head. "Fatima, I have an idea. Why don't we organize a candle-light vigil at the Commons on campus?"

"Yes, I like that idea. I know the athletes would do it. He was…is popular. I'll start writing down a plan."

"Good." Laura breathed a sigh of relief to hear calm restored in her voice. "Hang in there. I'll see you soon." She hung up, her mind already mulling over possibilities.

"You're planning a candlelight vigil?" Chase's sudden appearance made her jump.

She nodded. "With Fatima. I think that we all need to focus on a positive outcome."

Chase shrugged. He grabbed his jacket. "Ready."

"Chase, you're closing me out…again."

He stopped in front of her. She saw from the rigid set of his shoulders that she had hit a nerve. Maybe she was pushing his buttons, but she would rather a heated debate, than this cold detachment.

"We don't have to stay here to talk. We can talk on the way because I know that you're in a hurry to get to Ned," Laura said.

"No. Let's get whatever is on your mind out so that I can address it, once and for all."

"I don't understand your anger. Now. Today. After we—"

"We made love," he finished. "You've said that before."

"And you used Ned as your excuse." Laura was tired of taking the soft approach. She felt surrounded by people with emotional issues—Kasey and her brother's death, Fatima and her relationship with Ned, Chase and whatever brought this dark, brooding attitude.

"Don't say that. Ned is the reason why I thought about coaching. These young athletes today think that it's about who runs the fastest, or who jumps the farthest. Talent defines the athlete, but stamina determines the staying power."

"He's more than an athlete. He's a young man." Laura sensed that the conversation drifted between Ned's future and Chase's past.

Chase stared at her. The pain reflected in his eyes didn't match the lack of emotion on his face. She detested his ability to assume this iron man attitude.

"Hey, go see Ned. Then think about talking to someone." Laura's voice died away.

Chase backed away from her with an incredulous expression. "I don't need a shrink. I don't have a problem stating the obvious. Laura, I gave up everything to have this career. I put my heart into practicing, living and breathing my coach's advice. All that mattered is being the first one to break that tape. Then the injuries started. A minor muscle here and there, then it was muscle tears, then stress fractures, then torn ligaments. Slowly, my dreams evaporated and I had to face ending it all. That second chance is out there, but the odds are against it happening for me. And I could do irreparable damage even trying."

"But I've seen you training. I think it's all coming back if you'd let it."

"I thought I saw you out there. Well, now I know that Ned will be faced with even bigger odds. I don't know how to bring him back from the depression that I'm sure he'll experience. I'm not a walking success story. I feel as if I won't be there for him."

"Hey." She touched his arm. "You are his *coach*. But I think that before this is all over, Ned will need a team of not only doctors and physical therapists, but also probably psychotherapy to deal with some of his issues. His recovery is truly a medical team effort."

He touched her cheek gently, a sad smile on his face. "You and I used to be a team."

"I know that you want more from me than this."

"Right now having you in my life is more important. Laura, I love you."

Laura nodded. Her heart responded likewise, even though she couldn't quite say it.

Almost a month later, Laura drove into Hampton Mews, the city in Maryland that she once called home. She'd been gone for almost six months, but urban development continued to prosper. She drove past new shopping centers with light, frilly names like Sunrise Town Center and Bluebells Outlet Shopping District.

Large parcels of undeveloped land displayed signs for upcoming housing communities. The prices floored her since they were more than triple what their family home was worth. She had seen on the news and in papers that the Atlantic corridor, including Maryland, Virginia and Washington, D.C., had expensive homes that required owners with deep pockets. Who would have predicted their sleepy town nestled in a mountain valley would attract thousands of families?

Laura pulled up in front of Pierce's home. It was once the family home, the one that they had struggled to keep after their father left and then after their mother died. Pierce had done some work on the façade with a brighter paint, and if she wasn't mistaken, the porch had been redone. They'd all been glad that not only had Pierce moved into the house, but also that he'd finally settled down with a wonderful wife and stepdaughter.

Maybe now he could stay out of everyone else's business.

Laura ran up the front steps, with an overwhelming happiness. She'd promised to come home for Thanksgiving, but didn't tell them what day she'd arrive. It didn't matter. Once she flew in, she rented a car and drove to the house.

"Aunt Laura," Beth exclaimed. "You're here. Mom!"

"Girl, stop yelling," Laura scolded her niece.

Laura smiled as her new sister-in-law emerged from the kitchen with a pot spoon in one hand and an oven mitt in the other. "Oh my gosh, Laura? Girl, what are you doing here without calling any of us?" They hugged. Laura had bonded with Haley immediately, admiring her strength and perseverance with divorcing her husband, moving to a new town and dealing with her daughter's bumpy adjustment to everything.

"Where's my big brother?"

"At the office. He'll get in around six." Haley ran toward the kitchen. "Come talk to me while I flip these pieces of chicken. They need another coating of barbeque sauce."

"Homemade sauce?"

"But of course. How could anyone use barbeque sauce from the bottle?"

Laura kept her mouth shut. No need to confess her grave sin. At least she never bragged that she was a cook. She took a seat at the dinette table.

Beth chatted away about school and her new friends. Good news to see that she had settled down. Haley had to be pleased because she knew it was a burden to deal with the doubts and guilt of moving her.

"Beth, would you give Laura a break. She'll be here all week. When are you leaving?"

"Not until Saturday night. Don't want to deal with the Thanksgiving traffic at the airport. Plus it was cheaper if I left on Saturday."

"I hear you. You're looking fabulous. Lost weight. Wearing your hair longer. Makeup. Must be a man in the picture."

"Or I'm a successful African-American woman making her career as a physical therapist."

"Yeah, that, too. How's that going, by the way?"

"It's been an interesting couple of months. Lots of good has come out of the experience, but a couple of really horrendous things happened, too."

Haley set the tray of baked chicken on the range. She pulled off her glove, setting it on the counter. "Want to talk about it?" Haley pulled out a pitcher of lemonade and poured two glasses.

"Pierce will be home in less than an hour. We can wait for him or dig in now."

Laura took the glass of lemonade, grateful for the cool liquid quenching her thirst. "I'll wait. I miss having family dinners. Most of my dinners are spent heating up a frozen dinner and eating it in front of the TV." She laughed. "I sound like a real single woman."

"Yeah, because if you had a man, you'd be learning how to cook and fixing glorious meals."

"Very liberated, Haley. That's what you think." Laura rolled her eyes.

"Oh. Does your man know how to cook?" Haley pushed.

"I have a friend. No, he doesn't do the cooking. We order in."

"Where are the old-fashioned men?" Haley took a seat next to her, squeezing her hand. "I've missed seeing you. Even your sister, Sheena, and I have bonded, if you can imagine that one. You mentioned some bad things, though?"

Laura quickly explained about Ned. "Once he passed through the dangerous period after his surgery, they didn't know how quickly he would recover. His girlfriend organized a candlelight vigil, which drew several hundreds of students and people from the community. Ned was the center point, but we were all thinking about drunk driving, too. I'd like to think that our prayers and well wishes helped him."

"Can't imagine what his parents must have gone through."

Laura nodded. "Now he's in a wheelchair. He's determined to walk again, but the doctors say the prognosis is slim."

"They don't know crap. People shouldn't write off other people. He'll get that inner strength and surprise them one day."

Laura wanted to believe that, but she felt the same way as the doctors. Even Chase, didn't buy into her blind optimism. They kept their counsel on the matter not wanting to sound dismal.

"Is he home?"

"He's off campus, but goes to classes. He only takes one class a day and it wipes him out. His father pays for a nurse to accompany him. I suppose that it's keeping up his spirits. I want to do something for him, but I'm not sure what would be meaningful and still motivational."

"Well, maybe you'll get a chance to think about

it while you're here. No one to bother you. No stresses. No job. No man," Haley teased.

If she only knew that the man in discussion was right now at his family's house less than ten miles away. They had flown in together, but went their separate ways at her insistence. As much as they had called their truce, there were so many unanswered pieces in their relationship. She would have to deal with his snobby family. And she had to deal with Pierce's opinion of her reunion with Chase.

"Do you need me to show you to your room?"

"Nope. I'm in the bedroom next to the shower—right?"

"Yes. You'll like the new look," Haley said with pride.

Laura went upstairs, very curious to see Haley's creation. She certainly had turned up the notch with the home interior decorating, cooking and other home-based charms. Maybe some of her talent would rub off on her before she left.

The guest room happened to be the smallest room of the three bedrooms. Omar had his own room when Pierce declared that he was too old to have to share his room with his brother. Their mother didn't think twice and gave the bedroom to Omar, Pierce got the basement, while she and her sister, Sheena, shared a room. The girls were not happy and felt that their mother had betrayed them. Her mother's defense was that they needed more bonding than boys did.

Standing in the room looking around at the different decorations and furniture, Laura now understood that her mother relied on Pierce a lot for keeping them in line. The huge basement was his reward for not having the childhood she would have wanted for him.

Laura set down her luggage and sat on the bed. The room had been repainted from the garish blue that Omar had chosen to a soft muted peach with white trimmings. The furniture had a blond color that didn't overpower the room with its size or dark shade. A frilly curtain decorated the two windows that overlooked the side of the house.

Beth appeared in her doorway.

"Come in. I really missed you. How are your friends?"

Beth rolled her eyes. "I've been good. Those friends didn't care about me anyway. Once I stopped doing what they wanted, they didn't want to hang around me. I think they were scared of Pierce."

"He can be a scary guy. When we were younger, we plotted ways that we could outsmart him. Never worked. You know, I think that Omar probably told him everything we said because he always stayed one step ahead." Laura laughed at the memory.

"Wish that I had a brother or sister."

"I know, Sweetie. But you've got an uncle and two aunts, in addition to your mom's brothers." Laura hadn't touched the subject of children with Haley. Considering how old Beth was, she couldn't blame her if she didn't want to deal with diapers and formula again.

"I went to visit my father on Labor Day weekend."

"Really?" Laura couldn't hide her surprise, considering all the drama that Haley's ex had caused.

"Pierce talked to him. I eavesdropped." Beth smiled. "Mom didn't want Pierce to meet with him. But when he came back, he said there would be no problem from dad. Mom said that she wasn't going to push me to meet with him or even stay with him. It was all up to me."

"That must have been a big decision." Laura felt a little left out, not that her brother's family affairs should include her. Yet she was used to the all-member family meetings whenever one of them had a crisis. Now, she didn't get much as a phone call asking her opinion or anything.

"I thought about it a lot. Mom didn't bug me. I tried to get Pierce to tell me what to do, but he said that he couldn't do that. Then I called my dad. We had a long talk. I think that he might have been crying, but I was crying, too." She smiled up at Laura, her eyes shiny. "I felt better. I realized that I do want to see him." She waved her hands. "It all worked out."

Laura hugged her. "You are too cute and grown up."

"This is true."

A door slammed.

"Pierce is here!" Beth ran out of the room and down the stairs to her stepfather.

"So this is what it feels like to have a real family life." Laura headed downstairs to enjoy her first home-cooked meal in months. Her stomach echoed her sentiments as the smell of the baked chicken and other savory, tantalizing scents teased her.

Pierce stood in the living room while Beth blurted out the news of her arrival. Haley busily went back and forth, loading the table with food.

"Hey, big brother, what's up." They hugged longer than they normally would have. "How's the practice?"

"Now that I have a great office manager, it's running smoothly and I actually get home on time."

"Great. Hope it's someone that won't let you down," Laura warned.

"Not a chance," Beth piped up. "Mom is the office manager."

"Actually, I share the job with a retired teacher. It's working out great and I can be home more."

"That part sucks." Beth made a face.

"Let me go wash up and I'll join you all for dinner," Laura remarked.

They had gotten caught up on the local news, her workplace and a vague outline of Omar's goings-on. She managed to gloss over the fact that Omar was living with her while he pursued yet another career dream.

"Let's sit out on the deck. We can have coffee.

I made an angel food cake with fresh fruit compote," Haley bribed.

"Pierce, where is my sister-in-law? The one I left here with you, not this domesticated, whiz-in-the-kitchen woman. You're making me tired watching you."

"That's what happens when you're in love." Haley bent over and kissed Pierce on the lips.

Laura and Beth guffawed enjoying the embarrassing blush over her brother's face.

"Or when you're expecting," Pierce added.

"No way!" Laura hugged Haley and then stepped back afraid that she hugged too hard.

"No one thought I could keep a secret," Beth said proudly.

"Keeping secrets from your auntie is not good," Laura teased. "How far along are you?"

"Just hit the third month." Haley rubbed her flat stomach.

"On that note, I'm going to leave you ladies." Pierce excused himself.

"That's his excuse to do some work at home. I'm just glad he's here."

"Let's go drink that coffee. You, however, will have to drink milk."

Haley made a face, opting for another glass of lemonade. Beth ran off to work on a class project. Under a soft light, they sat in the enclosed deck enjoying the cool night air. Laura wore enough layers that the dip in temperatures didn't bother her.

"Funny how the small town life doesn't ever leave your blood. It really feels good to be back home to take a breather." Laura leaned back her head, smelling the faint whiff of the herbal garden that Laura had planted in window boxes at the kitchen windows.

"Life is funny. You can never figure it out regardless of how much you plan. Now I'm going to be a mommy again. I'm scared to death."

"Isn't everything okay?" Laura hoped that there were no health concerns.

"Everything is fine. It's been a while since I did this. Not that I've forgotten, but will I have the energy to run after a toddler? Will I become a screaming banshee of a wife and drive Pierce away?"

"You're making me want to move back and be here for you and my niece or nephew. Think I'd like a nephew. What do you think?"

"I'll see what I can do for you." Haley grinned. "So, I want to hear about Mr. Right."

Laura raised her eyebrow and with a straight face, she lied, "There's no Mr. Right."

"Hmm." Haley sipped her lemonade. "Who is Chase?" She pulled out a folded piece of paper and handed it to her.

Laura felt as if she had swallowed a golf ball. Chase contacted her once he arrived in Hampton Mews, but they had made no plans for the Thanksgiving holiday considering that she didn't want to see his family. And she wanted to discuss him with Pierce first.

"Don't look so mortified. I told him you were washing up and then we would be sitting down for dinner." She looked at her watch. "As a matter of fact, he said that he would come over around eight." The door bell chimed. "Punctual fellow. He's scored with me already." Haley beamed, clearly pleased with herself to deliver the surprising news.

Laura sprang out of the chair and ran into the kitchen, almost knocking herself out in the process as she maneuvered around the kitchen counter and dinette table. She saw Pierce heading toward the door. She turned up the speed and sprinted down the hallway, barreling into Pierce in the process. "Sorry," she gasped. "I've got the door."

"What is the hurry?" Pierce shook his head as if she had lost her mind.

"Nothing." She opened the door, but kept her body in the doorway waiting for Pierce to head back to the study. When he finally turned to walk away she turned to see Chase looking more than a little bewildered.

"Everything okay?" Chase asked.

"Sure. Just trying to beat Pierce to the door. Haven't chatted about everything to him, as yet." Laura tried to keep her voice low.

"That's why I thought I'd come over and get things out in the air."

"Maybe not." Now wasn't the time for him to be stubborn.

"Laura, why don't you invite your guest in?" Pierce hadn't gone into his study after all. And from the tone of his voice she knew that she was busted.

She scrunched her face, holding her breath. Now the drama would unfold.

Welcome back, Chase, she said to herself.

Chapter 10

Laura turned to face Pierce, hoping that he wouldn't make the night unbearable. It was only her first day back and already she had to deal with tension. That's what she got for putting off telling him about Chase.

"Come in, Chase," Pierce invited, no warmth in his tone.

Her brother looked over her head, his focus no longer on her. She stepped aside to allow Chase to fully enter the hall.

"Anyone for lemonade?" Not that she slowed

down to get their responses, but she needed a quick break to regroup. She heard Chase accept a drink. If Pierce answered, she didn't hear and wasn't about to go back and ask him to repeat.

"You don't look happy to see your young man." Haley peeped out toward the living room. "Looks like a respectable young man."

"We used to date. Then we broke up. Wasn't pretty."

"And everything is great now, right?" Haley turned from her vigil at the doorway to look at her.

"It's not good, it's not bad. We don't want to be away from each other. But any other type of commitment would be too much. Taking things slow." Laura pulled down three glasses from the overhead cabinets. She filled them with lemonade and ice.

"Oh." Haley started cleaning up the remaining dishes, loading them into the dish washer. "Don't you want more than that?"

Laura shrugged. She found a tray for the drinks and picked up her load to head back into choppy waters.

"I'm not done with you," Haley said to her retreating back.

Laura walked into the living room and offered Chase his drink. She could feel his gaze on her when she stood in front of him, but she kept her gaze slightly off to the side of his face. Then she turned to Pierce who looked calm. But too calm, alarming her. She noticed that the conversation stopped when she entered.

"Haley!" Pierce yelled. "I'd like my wife to meet you," he said to Chase.

Haley popped in. From where she was in the kitchen, there was no way that she would have arrived in the living room so quickly. She'd been waiting for this.

Chase didn't wait for Pierce to perform the introductions. He took the initiative and introduced himself. Haley's smile couldn't have gotten any wider.

"Laura, looks like you neglected to tell me that you were with Chase again," Pierce said matter-of-factly.

Laura hated when he went from brother to father role. She'd seen it done to her sister and brother, but she managed to keep his interference at a minimum. She was good at following the rules.

"Honey, she doesn't have to clear her relationships with you. I'm glad that we got to meet." Haley looked over at Laura and offered a conspiratorial wink.

"That's fine. Pierce likes to play the gatekeeper. Chase and I reconnected in Atlanta. Nothing more."

"And do you think this is wise, considering what happened previously?"

"We were younger then," Chase defended. "We're not rushing into anything."

"People change," Haley offered, but a worried frown marked her forehead. "May I ask why you all broke up?"

"I wasn't ready to make a commitment to a relationship and my career. I chose my career."

"Do you think that was the better choice?" Pierce challenged.

"Unfair!" Laura shouted. "Chase, don't answer that." She didn't want to hear his thoughts.

"Pierce." Haley's voice took on an edge.

"Why is this such a problem to talk about the real issues between you? I'm trying to make sure that you've settled it." Pierce turned to Laura. "You turned my sister's world upside down. Your family treated us like charity cases because we were marked by our father leaving the family. Then when Laura hooked up with you, they almost had a heart attack. Your mother said things to Laura and me, terrible things. Then, while you went off to grab that brass ring, our family picked up the pieces." He fixed Laura with a hard stare. "This is why I'd like to ensure that we don't have to sweep up his aftereffects once more."

"His mother spoke to you?" Laura had no idea.

"Yes. I defended my sister and family. But that didn't matter. Your mother was looking for purebred stock to carry on the legacy of the Westfields. After all, their thoroughbred son was on the fast track to being a celebrity athlete."

"I know my mother wasn't kind. I don't know to what extent she may have taken that attitude."

"Attitude! Try venom," Pierce corrected.

Chase nodded. "I wasn't in a position to be a husband to Laura."

"Who asked you to be a husband?" Laura's mouth fell open.

"That's what everyone expected, if not then at some time down the road.

"That's not really it," Pierce said. "You thought

that she would hold you back because of who she is." Pierce stared contemplatively at Chase. "Did your coach also steer you away from her, in case she wound up pregnant and you'd have that hanging around your neck?"

Laura stared at Chase wanting him to defend Pierce with a righteous anger that he wouldn't think that way. She'd known Chase before he was a name on the popularity list at school or the star at track and field events. They were young, she understood that, but she felt that their friendship would hold over until they were old enough to make serious decisions.

"I'm trying to make up for what I did. In order for me to do that I have to look in a forward direction. I can't change the past. I can apologize, but that doesn't fix the hurt. What would make you feel better about me, Pierce?"

"I don't really know. You haven't been at the top of my thoughts. As a matter of fact, I never thought that I'd see you again once you left Hampton Mews."

"I'm going to step in here." Haley stood up and actually stepped in the circle, turning around so everyone could see her face. "This visit I'm sure hasn't turned out the way any of us envisioned. This is Thanksgiving weekend and I want us to put our differences aside. I'm not saying that we sweep things out of sight. We've all got a lot to be thankful for and that's what I want us to focus on. Chase, you are welcome to share Thanksgiving dinner with us."

"Thank you. I'll let you know. My family is also having dinner."

"Notice, he didn't invite us," Pierce taunted.

Laura cringed at her brother's half-joking, sarcastic comment.

"Pierce, enough!" Haley glared at her husband.

Laura also stood, seeing that Chase was ready to leave. She motioned with her head that she would follow him. They walked out onto the porch. Laura closed the front door to separate Pierce and Haley, already in heated discussion, from Chase and her.

"I could have told you it wasn't the right time," Laura began.

"I don't think any time would have been the right time. I had to take the chance. I'd say that being grilled by your brother is like walking over hot coals. But I'd be that ferocious if my sister needed me."

Laura wanted to conduct her form of grilling. What was she afraid of? There could be nothing of substance between them if they didn't or couldn't talk about the heavy stuff that stood between them.

"Don't lose confidence in me," Chase requested.

"Honestly, I'm trying not to. I think that we have to reconnect as friends, gain each other's trust before anything else can be expected. I know that you told me that you loved me. I know you're not being frivolous with your emotions. But loving doesn't mean that I'm right for you."

He kissed the top of her forehead. "I hate to leave you to deal with Inquisition Part II, but I have to run."

"You don't have to come to dinner." Laura didn't mean it. She really wanted him to show Pierce that he was man enough to stand in front of him—imperfections and all.

"We'll see." Chase didn't meet her eyes.

Chase's house had been the envy of his childhood classmates. His father, an architect by profession, had designed their Tudor mansion at the height of his career. His mother was a Ph.D. in Pan-African Philosophy and a renowned writer for various scholarly journals. This was his frame of reference with nothing to compare it to.

Chase pulled into the driveway leading to the garages in the rear of the property. Pierce thought that he felt superior because of his family's money. Maybe he did feel that way, if he could push Laura away from him whenever people reminded him of his potential. Of his past. Of his future.

"Hi, son," his mother greeted. She wore royal blue and gold colors and was bedecked with pearls.

"Sorority function, huh?" he asked.

"We are feeding the homeless. I should be home around six. Let's chat about Thanksgiving dinner and what will be on the menu. Your cousins, aunts and uncles haven't seen you in so long that we are going to have a huge Thanksgiving celebration."

He duly kissed her cheek and watched her head out the door to her jet-black luxury sedan. She was always the same, and would be horrified to think that there were people who didn't like her—she had done the damage to her own image.

What people didn't understand about her was her big heart. Once a person was in need, she'd hurry at break neck speed to help them. She did tend to brag about her contributions, but then everyone had some weakness or the other.

But why had she been so cruel to Laura and her family?

Chase stayed to himself most of the evening. His father usually spent his time in his office working around the clock. As the evening got later, Chase walked around turning on the lights. The house that used to be so full of life, seemed quiet as if he'd stepped in a library or museum. His father's office door opened. He emerged in his khakis and buttoned up golf shirt.

"Did your mother make dinner?" his father asked, heading toward the kitchen.

Chase was about to say no when he spied the covered plate near the range. His mother and father lived such old-fashioned lives. But he'd take his 1950s father era over one like Laura's, who had walked out.

"Are you going to stand over me? Join me. I can't imagine that your mother didn't leave a plate for you." His father offered to share.

"I'm not feeling particularly hungry." Chase's stomach hadn't stopped its nervous rumbling since he returned from Laura's. "Mom announced that she was having a big spread for Thanksgiving. She invited the aunts and uncles."

"It's all for you." His father grinned. Pierce didn't miss the humorous twinkle behind his bifocals. "You know everyone is excited with the accomplishments you've made. How are you doing, though? Tried not to bother you with questions after the injury."

"My body is mending. But I haven't pushed myself. I'm a little hesitant to take my body to the max. Feels like the window of opportunity on my comeback is closing in front of me." Chase didn't mind sharing his vulnerability with his father. Joseph Westfield was the strong, silent type, not given too many emotional displays. Yet he was a good listener and patient counselor, especially during Chase's teens. Unfortunately, he'd been tarnished by his wife's reputation for being judgmental and impulsive with her criticism. The poor man had gotten his guilty verdict by association.

"Then why are you at the university wasting valuable time?"

"Wasting? I thought you'd be appreciative of my stable, normal job." Chase couldn't have been more surprised.

"Not at all. I do the stable, normal things so that you could achieve your dreams without worrying. If you feel that you've got something in that reserve tank, I say let it rip."

"And I thought mom was the stage mother in the family," Chase joked.

"I'm not the type that pushed for my approval. If you fell flat on your face, well, then you learned what not to do again."

"Well, I'm tired of coming up with the right choices, Dad. My life is going off in various directions. I'm stumped as to which road to take."

His father nodded. Chase had heard all his life that he was the spitting image of his father. Only their body types differed. Maybe since his father had never pursued athletics, but was a brilliant scholarly type, they didn't carry the same build. Chase, unlike his father, wouldn't dress for dinner, coming to the table in sweats, jeans or slacks. In contrast, his mother and father would sit at their table looking as if they were heading out on a date.

His father cleared his throat. "What's your biggest fear, son?"

"That I'd risk injuring myself in the trials."

"But that could've happened before. Why is that bothering you now?"

"I don't want to go for the gold with everything that I've got, sacrifice so much, and then not get it."

"You've never been this scared before," his father remarked.

"True, but now I know how much I lost by going for the ultimate prize. Not sure if it's worth it again."

His father zoned again, frowning over whatever thoughts entered his head. Chase didn't know whether the conversation was over, since they weren't talking. But it wouldn't be unusual for his father to seek him out later that evening and continue as if they hadn't ever paused.

He heard the garage door open. His mother had returned home. If she got wind of this conversation, he would be stuck at that dining table all night until he surrendered to her wishes, whatever they were. Chase got up to help her with whatever shopping she'd done. Since she had

been gone for most of the day, he knew that she'd
have two bags per every hour that she was out of
the house.

The door opened. His mother appeared with
the gaudiest coat that he'd ever seen. She must be
roasting under that full length leather. His mother
would suffer discomfort if it meant that she
thought that she was looking darn good after
looking in the mirror. He didn't see her leave with
it, so it was probably a recent purchase. November
was usually cold, but the Thanksgiving weekend
promised to be warm.

"So glad you're here, Sweet Pea. I have a few
bags in the back of the car. Could you do your
mother a kind favor and get them for me?"

"Sure." Some things never changed. Susan
Westfield always felt that she could dupe him into
manual labor with childish names like Sweet Pea.
It had gotten him into many near fights when she
chose to call him that in front of his friends.

Chase went to the car and almost ran back into
the house. If training didn't injure his knee, lifting
the ten bags of food items would certainly do it.
He didn't need to ask to know that this was for
the Thanksgiving meal. He thought of the huge

numbers coming with their probing questions, hidden agendas and aggressive nosiness.

After several trips from the car to kitchen, he heard bits and pieces of conversation that involved the invitation list. His mother could invite the entire neighborhood and it wouldn't matter. He planned on changing his flight and heading back to Atlanta on Friday after the dinner. Regardless of his decision, and he was no closer to making one, he had to talk to his coach—man to man.

In the best case scenario, he could whisk Laura away, tell her his fears and listen to her perspective. If she thought that he should go for that ultimate prize, then he'd know that he was doing it with her blessing. Ultimately, that seemed to be the only thing that could soothe his conscience.

"How about the Mastersons? They were his friends. Maybe he'd like to see them at dinner," his father said.

"I don't know if that's necessary for the party. I think Chase can see them informally."

"But it's not a formal dinner. I like talking to Pierce," his father countered.

"You haven't talked to Pierce in a very long time." His mother's speech got slower, a sign of her increased irritation. She didn't like obstacles and his father's defense of the Mastersons was proving to be a difficult issue. Chase remained where he was, wondering how this would end.

"See, that's where you're wrong. I went to see Pierce about my lower back pain the other day."

"What lower back pain? You didn't tell me," his mother actually sputtered. "Why on earth would you go to Pierce? He's too young to know anything."

"Pierce is a good doctor who came highly recommended from *your* friends. I went to him because I figured that I didn't need your permission." Way to go, Dad, Chase thought. Lots had definitely changed since his last extended visit.

Chase rested the last bag of groceries down as gingerly as possible. His mother wasn't the type to throw a fit. She would walk away and just not speak for an entire day. Then inevitably, he or his father would make a grand apology and wait for her forgiveness. They'd done the routine so many times that it had become habit. Now dad had openly defied her and she hadn't collapsed from the shock.

Figuring that the time was right to make his

entrance, Chase popped his head into the dining room. "Since you're having a discussion on invitees, I wanted to let you know that the Mastersons are having their own Thanksgiving dinner. Maybe we could have them, or Laura, over on Wednesday, instead."

His mother shifted her angry gaze from his father to him. "I'm not having two dinners and not especially for the Mastersons. Anyway, I'm not keen on any of the sisters."

"Sheena and Laura," Chase reminded.

His mother's mouth formed a firm line, refusing to utter those names.

"Well, the kicker to all of this is that Laura and I are dating, again."

His mother pulled out a chair to sit.

Even his father looked surprised before a wide grin erupted. "Laura's back in the picture? It's okay, honey. He's a big boy."

"I'm disappointed in you, Chase, for springing that on me in this manner," his mother fretted. "Dinner plans will not be changed. I'm going to relax because I suddenly have a headache." With that, she made a dramatic exit past the two men. Chase heard her sharp footsteps against the uncarpeted steps as she walked to her room overhead. Then a door slammed. His father may have to get his pillow and move to one of the guest rooms for the night or two.

"I'll be in my study," his father remarked, disappearing behind closed doors.

Chase headed for the family room. It looked like the TV would be up for grabs. However, instead of turning on the TV, he aimed his remote at the stereo system and played his favorite station featuring soft jazz. This is how Chase remembered spending many nights with his father. They'd gone to several Caribbean islands, St. Lucia being their favorite, to attend summer jazz festivals. He missed those days.

His father reappeared in the family room. "Slide over." He sat next to Chase and propped his legs on the leg-rest. "Didn't feel like working. So, tell me about Laura."

"I'd planned to tell you without the dramatics."

"Not a problem. You don't have to convince me of Laura. She grew up to be a beautiful girl, both inside and out."

"I agree." Chase wanted to share the true nature of the relationship and the underlying reason. His father would be very upset upon hearing how Laura and her brother felt about their family. At some point they'd have to talk about it. He wanted Laura in his life. His mother's approval would be nice, but unnecessary.

The station played a string of George Benson hits, providing the perfect background for a father-son chat. He looked over at his father nodding his head to the slow, bluesy vibes. This felt good.

"Do you think that Laura will be the one?"

Chase was surprised at the direct question. "I want it to be. Did you know right away that mom was the one?"

"Yep, every morning when I rode my bike delivering papers, she'd have an excuse to be outside. Her brothers tried to beat me up when I stopped to talk to her, once. But I persisted. I saved all my money and sneaked into one of the dances wearing my cheap suit. We were chatting and dancing on the porch outside when one of the old biddies saw us. She went and told your grandmother. Not only was I banned from seeing your mother, but I lost my paper route, and my mother lectured me about embarrassing her with those high fallutin' girls." His father chuckled heartily. "And now look at us. One big happy family." This time, they both shared a laugh. "Guess it's getting late. Time for me to go upstairs and get my butt whipped."

"Holler if you need me." Chase laughed at his father's exaggerated, dragging gait.

Chase didn't worry about his parents. They never had arguments or disagreements that degenerated into disrespectful altercations. Even in their discussions, they maintained a certain air of diplomacy or manners. He did get a chuckle from seeing his father being more outspoken though.

What a revelation his father laid on him. The similarities between what his father experienced with his mother and her family were eerily similar to Laura's feelings. His father could look back and chuckle because of the happy ending, but now he truly understood how Laura must have felt. He shuddered to think that his self-absorption didn't allow him to see his mother's manipulation or his tunnel vision.

Chase returned to his bedroom in the basement. As a teen, he made the formal request to remove his belongings to the empty guest room in the basement. His mother didn't agree, initially. Pressure from him and his uncles about him needing his space and growing up to be a man, not a mama's boy, forced her to change her mind. However, she created a laundry list of don'ts that had to be obeyed.

Yet with all his mother's idiosyncrasies and her snobbish attitude, he suspected that she only did it out of love—controlling love—but love, nevertheless. The image of Laura and his mother together under the same room couldn't take form in his head. He had a better shot at the Olympic gold, than Laura and his mother going on a shopping spree together.

Thinking about Laura, he called her. Disappointed that she didn't answer, he waited for the voicemail and left a quick message.

Fifteen minutes later, the phone rang.

"You called?" Laura asked.

"Yep. Thinking about you."

"Same here." Laura sighed.

"Told my parents about us."

A loud crash of an approaching thunderstorm sounded overhead.

"Whoa. I'll take that as a sign of how that discussion ended. You don't sound upbeat. No need to ask how it went."

"Remember how we used to sneak out and go to the ninety-nine cents movies."

"In that crappy theater." Laura laughed. "We'd get a big tub of their stale popcorn and sneak in our sodas. Those were the good days."

"You want to go a movie with me." He yearned for those easier times, when plotting how they would be together was the most difficult decision to be made. "We can sneak in our sodas."

"Only if we go to the new mega movie complex. I have no desire to worry about mice running past my feet while I'm watching the movie."

"That only happened to you once." Chase tried to bite back his laugh.

"Keep it up and you'll be watching the movie alone," Laura threatened.

"Do you want me to pick you up?"

"No, I'll pick you up. What are we going to see?"

"There's a horror flick or a chick flick."

"Aren't you the Neanderthal calling a movie a chick flick?"

"I wasn't the one who gave it that title," Chase protested. "I would love to see the movie that is for and about women. I want to get in touch with your high level of estrogen."

"You're just the freaking comedian tonight."

"Okay, see you in an hour. I'll have our stash available. By the way, Chase, pack an overnight bag. I'm not returning you home until tomorrow," Laura teased with a husky, sexy voice before hanging up.

Chase's mind reacted to the promise. He'd dared to hope that they could find time together over the break. Sneaking her into his room in the basement wouldn't be cool. Or being with Laura on the same floor with her brother had a certain ick factor. He happily stuffed underwear, toiletries and a change of shirt into a small duffle bag. Nothing better than having a road trip with a beautiful bombshell.

Unlike his younger days when he sneaked out, this time he left a note on the refrigerator that he'd be back tomorrow. His mother would have to make another retreat to her bedroom after she saw it.

Chapter 11

"What did you think?" Laura asked, curious to hear Chase's reaction to the movie.

"Wasn't bad. But the whole love story was a little hokey. Why would he fall in love with her? She was like psycho queen."

"Because love can go beyond our mental barriers and perception." Laura knew that he hated getting into a debate with her. He'd accused her that her demeanor changed as if she was gearing up for a sparring match. She dismissed his protests. Inevitably she always won, which was the key reason why debating was fun. "Don't you believe that you have mental barriers prohibiting you from accomplishing goals?" She glanced over, interested to hear his thoughts.

Chase frowned, but didn't respond.

"I'll share if you share," she nudged.

"No."

Laura didn't say anything further. She drove out of the city limits, heading back into the city of Fredrick. The streets were fairly busy for a place that she didn't consider the hot bed of night life. As cars passed, she saw that they were the pre-college and college age kids, hanging out at restaurants and eateries. She turned down a few streets until she saw the building ahead.

"Not that I'm complaining, but why did we drive almost an hour from home to come to a hotel?" Chase asked, looking a bit perplexed.

"The hotel was built last year. It's not a chain. The owner is strategically selecting small cities to place these hotels which have been featured in architectural and interior design magazines."

"Boutique hotels that cost a fortune in the middle of the city. Yeah that makes sense." Chase leaned forward to look out his window.

"What's your beef? I'm the one footing the bill. I didn't want us running into anyone in town. I also didn't want one of the regular hotels. This is special. We are escaping, as adults, to have wild, passionate sex. That should excite you, if nothing else." Laura rolled her eyes. Where was the romantic flavor, especially after deliberately watching a romantic movie? Now she was irritated.

"We could have had wild, passionate sex in my basement."

"Oh, that's really a throwback. Let's feel like oversexed teens. Now that's romantic! Geez, let me get my quarter for the condom machine." Laura was ready to get out of the car, but Chase still sat staring straight ahead. They hadn't said much after she picked him up and they headed to the movie theater. Maybe she'd missed a cue that he wasn't really excited about tonight.

Laura decided to try a different approach. She wasn't giving up on her night of passion. "How's work?"

"Huh." He turned, looking startled at the topic. "Why are we talking about work?"

"Can't talk about jumping your bones. So I'm

trying to connect and the only other thing that I know about is your work, unless you'd like to bring up a subject that you feel comfortable discussing." Her passion thermometer was taking a serious dive and she was beyond irritable.

"Work is fine. One of the sportswear companies is making a strong bid to be our official athletic wear."

"That's big. That also means that the college sports are doing well. Congrats," she complimented, encouraged that he was placing the university on the map.

"We're fairly decent. In recent years, we've had a few strong talents sign on. The track team will be phenomenal in another year."

"Because of Ned?" Laura had a soft spot for the young man given his recent string of bad luck.

"He's a strong factor, but not the only factor."

Laura looked up when Chase didn't continue. She'd come to realize that Ned was a sensitive subject. Since his long stay in the hospital, he'd finally been discharged with a long battery of physical therapy sessions awaiting him. Before the Thanksgiving break, they'd learned of his desire to come back to school on a part-time basis.

He also wanted to assist with the team in whatever capacity. Everyone knew that he needed the interaction to keep his spirit positively focused and strong.

"I think it'll do you some good to see Ned back on campus," Laura said.

Chase nodded. "That young man still has some fight in him."

"I agree. But track isn't everything. If his body isn't ready or won't ever be ready, he's got to also consider what else is out there for him."

"And only he can do that."

Laura caught the warning that Chase tossed at her. Did he think that she would interfere with Ned's head? First, she didn't have that type of relationship with Ned. Second, she believed in everything she just said. And she thought Chase, of all people, would understand.

Laura started the car and shifted the gear into reverse.

"Where are you going?"

"Home. I think it's safe to say that we're not going to be whispering sweet nothings in each other's ear."

"That's a first. Laura Masterson has called it

quits without a fight." Chase was looking at her with a mischievous gleam. "I wasn't going to make your kidnapping and ravaging of my body an easy thing. What kind of man do you think I am?" He leaned over and kissed the tip of her nose. "Turn off the ignition and let's get busy."

As she put the car into Park, Laura shook her head as she watched Chase cross the parking lot to the hotel's entrance with his duffel bag swinging at his side. Just when she thought that she had him all figured out, he went and did something totally crazy, and in this case, say something incredibly sexy.

The front doors swooshed open upon her approach. The lobby took her breath away. She stopped to look up and around the expansive area. From the outside, the hotel had a traditional structure of any other hotel. The interior with its soft clay and beige colors soothed her with its muted tones. The outside world with its hustle and bustle and loud people and colors were barred from entering.

From where she stood, she could see an interior courtyard with several little covered gazebos dotting the English garden. The setting was aptly suited for relaxing in the protected outdoors with a book. Although it was now dark outside, the area was well lit.

She looked over at Chase, who'd walked farther into the lobby, to admire the high ceiling that featured a fresco painting of a southwest desert landscape. She surmised that he had learned an appreciation for unusual designs from his architect father. She'd read that the owner lived in New Mexico and wanted to introduce the beauty of the southwest landscape into other parts of the country.

"Sorry." Laura noticed the hotel clerk waiting to address her. "I'm still admiring your hotel."

"Not a problem. Most of our guests are blown away when they enter the building for the first time." The hotel clerk made quick work of registering her and handing her the door keys.

They rode up the elevators which had not been neglected in the interior decorating plans. Marble floors and paneled walls continued the elegance with elaborate gold-covered wall sconces.

Chase held the elevator door for her to exit. He almost bumped into her because she'd stopped short to admire the floor. Large displays of silk flowers and cacti plants with a small rock water-fall as a centerpiece added to the feeling of having stepped into an atrium. They followed the signs for the room.

"You can do the honors." Laura handed the key card to Chase.

He opened the door, stepped in to hold it for her. They both stared at the expansive suite, which had to be the size of two and half typical hotel rooms. Laura had used a grand opening special that allowed her a discounted rate. There was no way that she could afford it otherwise.

Another way she and Chase had always been different.

"I think that we may have to stay here for two nights," Chase declared, as he inspected the rooms.

"I wish, but my sister-in-law and your mother would kill us if we disappeared on Thanksgiving Day."

"I know, but it'd be so much fun."

Laura kissed him lightly on the lips, glad to see that his mood had lightened. Playing hooky from their families would be fun in the short term and painful in the long term. She knew better than to set Pierce's nose out of joint in an attempt to be rebellious. But she was resolute. Eventually, he'd have to come around to her and Chase being together, for however long it lasted.

"Let's go check out the bathtub." Chase pulled her toward it.

"Probably resembles a small swimming pool."

They walked into the bedroom, marveling at the peach and burnt orange décor. The bathroom was behind a thick beveled glass wall where the person's shape would appear diffused.

"I think that I may need a snorkel for this tub," Chase joked.

Laura kicked off her shoes and stepped into the tub to test the depth. The highest side of the tub when she sat was just below her shoulders. Silver jet spouts lined the bottom and sides. She couldn't wait to take a bath, relaxing under the pulsating water massaging her back and legs.

"What are you looking at?" She made her way over to Chase who was busy in a small refrigerator.

"There's champagne in here. Did you order this?"

Laura nodded. "I figured that we'd celebrate

getting back together." Chase kissed her squarely on the lips, giving her a deep hug. They stayed in each other's arms simply enjoying the moment.

"Last one in the tub gets to be on the bottom in the bed," Laura said. She pulled off her top, but lost a few seconds with her stubborn bra.

Meanwhile, Chase didn't lose a beat. He pulled down his shorts and underwear in one tug, gathered his socks and shoes and tossed everything to the side. Then he pulled off his shirt, delayed by the buttons. Laura thought she saw a couple pop off, but she was too busy fighting with her watchband.

"That's why I bought waterproof for situations such as this." He ran past her and promptly jumped into the empty tub.

Laura wasn't far behind. She turned on the faucet, allowing more hot water to fill the tub. He'd soon figure out that she was boiling him. Until then, she'd enjoy the view of his naked body.

He motioned for her to come in. She stopped the water for safety's sake. To tease her, he turned around as if sporting the latest suit on the runway. And with a body like that, no wonder he was a sports model.

Maybe if he had stayed in the game as a professional track star, endorsements would have continued to catapult him to the sexy list based on his looks. Then he'd be definitely way out of her league, playing with the celebrity women who loved virile athletes on their arm.

"The water isn't going leap out of the tub and bathe you," Chase remarked, impatiently.

"You're in such a hurry all of a sudden. Minutes ago, I felt like I needed a crowbar to pry you from the seat."

"I wasn't used to being manhandled. Now I'm ready. I can't wait to be on the top." He helped her into the tub. "As a matter of fact, I'd like to be on the top over here." He pointed to a tiled area on the side of the tub. "Then over there." He pointed to the chaise lounge. "Then over there." He pointed to the bed.

"Always going for the second and third helpings," Laura teased. Each place that he pointed to provided vivid images of their bodies intertwined in heavy foreplay. Chase was a master in seduction, priming her body for the onslaught of their lovemaking. They had both learned from each other in their early courtship. She had no regrets with falling in love with the first man who sexually awakened her. And very little had changed since then.

She took a seat on a flat ledge built on the inside of the tub, which raised her body above the water line. The water lapped under her breasts, which reacted to the cool air temperature. Chase's eyes appreciatively swept over her breasts and up to her face. Desire smoldered in his gaze, and she was sure that she reciprocated with hers. He approached her, locking her between his arms. Their mouths met, kissing and releasing, sighing, laughing, nibbling.

The only sound audible was their heavy breathing in the midst of the curling steam around them. Laura looked into Chase's eyes, wishing that they were truly windows to his soul. Despite his teasing, she sensed some part of him had tucked away, had withdrawn from her. Then she may not hold up to equal scrutiny, knowing that she had to work hard not to fully give her heart to him. It hurt that she loved him, but she was too afraid to let herself go.

Hugging him tighter, she closed her eyes and surrendered to his deep kiss. His hands moved over her body, with only the water as an invisible barrier. He stroked her nipples, cupping her breasts to raise them out of the water toward his mouth.

"Let's skip #1 and #2 and go to #3." Laura motioned to the bed, her voice husky with desire.

"Your wish, my lady." He lifted her from the tub and carried her to the bed. Laura grabbed a few towels.

"I want you to dry me off. Every inch." Once she had a towel around her, she grabbed another. "I'll do you, first." She dragged the towel down his buffed chest, along his rippled stomach to his tapered waist and farther down. He caught her wrist in a surprisingly firm grip. "I won't be responsible if you go there."

"But I want every inch of you dry."

He sucked in air between his teeth. She took the towel and gently rubbed past his hips toward his arousal. He flinched, sucking in more air. "Nope. Can't play your game. You're making me cross-eyed."

"Let me show you what I was going to do." She leaned back onto the bed. Taking her towel, she wiped herself, deliberately playing the peek-a-boo game with her breasts. She saw the muscles in his stomach tighten and relax whenever her hand brushed her breast.

Then she wiped each side of her stomach, each time getting closer to below her waist line. His eyes dropped to where the towel was loosely draped across her hips. She opened her arms to welcome his beautiful chest touching hers and slid open her legs to welcome the rest of him.

Enough with the games. She wanted him rough and ready.

Laura enjoyed her Thanksgiving with her family. Her sister Sheena and her husband, Carlton, made their appearance. Her nephew had gone to his grandmother's who took him to Florida to visit the various theme parks. Laura sensed a few strained moments between Sheena and Carlton. Sheena wasn't the type of person that tolerated anyone interfering in her personal space, including Pierce. They had gone toe to toe many times. And Sheena was usually the victor.

After the dishes were cleared, Pierce and his brother-in-law played video games along with Beth. Laura could hear the trash talk among them. From the sounds of things, Beth was hurting the older men, and she wasn't afraid to rub their noses in it. The Masterson genes were rubbing off on her.

Laura looked at the large amount of dirty dishes piled on the various counters and table. Thank goodness she had Sheena and Haley or else she wouldn't have volunteered to wash dishes or stack them in the dishwasher.

"Why do we always get the clean up job?" Sheena complained.

"Would you rather go play with Beth, so she could whip on you?" Laura asked, with a laugh. "Plus this gives us a chance to catch up. I've already caught up with Haley."

"Not exactly," Haley interrupted. "I'm still waiting to hear more about Chase."

"Chase!" Sheena stopped in midstride with a greasy dish of sweet potato soufflé remnants. "You're seeing him again?" She placed the dish close to the sink and leaned in toward Laura. "When were you going to tell me?"

"She didn't exactly tell us," Haley explained. "He popped over to see his sweetheart."

"Pierce must have had a cow. Why didn't you call me, Girl?" Sheena turned to Haley.

Laura had made a big mistake in thinking that she could depend on Haley. Obviously, these two had done some bonding in her absence. Now instead of grilling Sheena, she had turned into the prime target.

"That explains the brightness about her." Sheena walked around her, sizing her up. "Remember how she'd wear those dull colors with her hair all droopy and plain. No oomph."

Laura ignored both of them. Their ribbing provided the perfect motivation to get the dishes done as quickly as possible.

"Once we get through these dishes, let's head to the porch," Sheena suggested.

"We can sit on the deck." Haley motioned toward the back door.

"The deck is boring. Why would I want to sit on the deck and watch the grass grow, when I could go on the porch and see what your fast busybody neighbors are up to? Plus that Mr. Coles likes to look at me." Sheena pranced around the kitchen.

"That man is as old as dirt. You ought to be ashamed exciting that man's heart," Laura admonished.

"At least there would be someone to appreciate the goods." Sheena continued with her task of packing away leftovers and carrying the dishes to the sink.

No one said anything. Laura wanted to ask her to elaborate, but there didn't seem to be a need for an explanation based on her words. Her sister's marriage had never been a smooth one.

Haley wiped down the table. Then she stacked the wine glasses that didn't go into the dishwasher. Laura focused on cleaning up one of the last serving dishes. Sheena had her back to them while looking out the back door.

After they'd finished, the women headed for the porch, figuring that they would be more comfortable in the various chairs.

"I want to hear about *you*, Sheena." Laura knew she would have to spill her story on Chase, but Sheena's case was more serious.

"Don't have anything substantive to tell you. Carlton's going through some type of midlife crisis. He said that he's not feeling fulfilled with his job, but he doesn't know what he wants to do. Guess I'm not satisfying him at home since I'm also on the list of things that don't fulfill him."

"Carlton, the one sitting in there, said that?" Laura wanted to march into the family room and demand an explanation from her brother-in-law, soon to be deceased if she had anything to say about it. He'd never gotten back in the family's good graces when he was laid off, then sat at home and spent the money. Sheena had worked two jobs. Pierce had to bail them out of the various jams.

"Before we get too hasty, maybe there's something at work that's causing him a lot of pressure. It can happen." Haley nodded toward Laura for support.

Laura didn't want to comply. She hated hearing the hurt in her sister's voice.

"There could be some*one* at work," Sheena said.

"I'm going to kick that man's butt." Laura sprang from the chair. The nerve of the man to come to Pierce's house to sit and eat like an innocent.

"Laura, sit down. Sheena, do you know that for sure?"

Sheena shook her head. Her face turned miserable.

Laura knew that Sheena had to have reached a critical point to open up with them. She knelt beside her sister's chair and wrapped her arms around Sheena's waist. She squeezed her, letting her know that she could depend on her.

"Sheena, are you ready?" Carlton stood at the doorway, looking down at them.

Sheena nodded. "Still want to hear about Chase," she whispered in Laura's ear.

Laura giggled. Compared to her sister's marital issues, her concerns with Chase paled.

Laura couldn't meet her brother-in-law's eyes. All she needed was a twitch of an eyebrow or smirk on his lips and she'd be all over him like a pitbull on a rampage.

Haley and Laura watched them drive off. Pierce and Beth had already resumed their fighting positions announcing their achievement to the next level of the video game.

"What was that all about?" Laura turned to Haley. "I know that you know. Come on, tell me."

"She suspected that he's having an affair. She doesn't have definite proof, but he's been acting weird lately, so she hired a private detective. Nothing definitive yet has been reported."

"They've been married for so many years." Laura had grown up in a broken home, but she couldn't help believing that marriages were supposed to last until death do you part.

"People sometimes outgrow their partners or they were never in love with their partner in the first place."

Laura had heard all about Haley's problems in her first marriage. At least there was hope that, if it didn't work out for Sheena, she didn't have to cut herself off from all relationships forever. Hopefully it wouldn't come to that. Laura loved her family and extended family. She didn't like to think of a marriage dissolving.

"I'm bushed. I'm heading for bed. It's been a long day." Haley yawned and stretched.

"It was a great dinner, Haley." Laura hugged her, then followed her into the house.

"Invite Chase over for lunch tomorrow," Haley suggested. "I think we should get to know him, don't you?" Laura nodded, beaming over Haley's non-judgmental kindness.

Laura pulled out her cell phone, returning to the deck. She didn't feel like going in just yet. She dialed Chase's number. Impatiently, she listened to

it ring before going into the voicemail system. After
the beep, she left her message for him to call her
back.

A thought popped into her head. She grabbed
her keys and headed for her car. He'd stopped by
to see her, knowing that he stood the chance of
meeting her brother. It didn't stop him. She felt
inclined to do the same with his family. Wouldn't
he be surprised? She grinned, happy with herself
for the impromptu visit.

The ride took about fifteen minutes due to a couple traffic lights. Standing in front of the door, she
was very nervous. Time to suck it up. She inhaled
to give herself a boost before pushing the doorbell.
Instantly, she wondered if this had been a good idea.

The door opened. Chase's father stared back at
her, momentarily speechless.

"Hi, Mr. Westfield, I stopped by to see Chase
and to wish you a Happy Thanksgiving."

"Come in, Laura. It's been a while since I last
saw you. Still pretty as ever."

"Joseph, who's at the door?"

The sound of Chase's mother approaching had
her stomach in somersaults. Please let Chase be
home, she begged to herself.

"It's Laura. She came to see Chase."

There was a pause in the approach. Then she'd resumed walking, much slower as a reflection of her enthusiasm. When she walked in the room, Laura resisted the urge to curtsy and lower her gaze until the queen commanded otherwise.

"Yes, Laura. How may we help you?"

"Chase." Laura fumed. Her husband just told her why she was there. It wasn't to sell cookies, that was for sure.

"You haven't changed much." Mrs. Westfield's mouth curled in distaste.

"So your husband said. Pretty were your words, right, Mr. Westfield?" She turned toward him and caught his small laugh before his wife's glare made it disappear.

"Joseph, weren't you busy? I'll chat with Laura…alone."

"Nice seeing you, Laura. Stop by whenever you want. I'd love to catch up with you and hear about what you're up to."

Chase's mother waited until her husband left, before turning to Laura. "Have a seat."

"I'd rather stand. I'm not planning to stay long."

"And you wouldn't be. Chase isn't here."

"What?" Laura looked for signs that his mother was joking or lying. "He's left to go back to school?" Laura was having trouble grasping the reality.

"Same scenario, different time, I'd think that you would've learned by now how important his professional track career is. His coach has been waiting for three months to get a final decision about his plans to return to the field. Like before, he had to suffer through distractions before making the right decision."

Chase's mother gave Laura a pitying look. "You didn't have a clue? I don't understand why you'd willingly put yourself between Chase and his dreams. Even if he thought that he could have both options at this time in his life, he'd come to resent you if he missed trying for the gold. I want the best for my son. The best, Laura."

Laura thought she would throw up right there. How could this happen again? The last time, he'd told her that he couldn't deal with a relationship, not even a friendship, so that he could put everything into his career. His mother had provided the encore, telling her about not being good enough to be a part of their family, even if he weren't a star athlete. The time had come to end all ties to the Westfield family for good.

"You've done a number on his head, young lady. He agonized in a way that doesn't warm my heart toward you. Once again, *I* had to reiterate the priorities in his life. You'd think he would have learned from the first time. Look how successful he became without any undue attachments. He did it once and I'm sure that he can do it again. Someday, you'll see that I'm right. When you become a mother you'll understand."

Laura willed herself not to cry. Her humiliation hung thick and tightly woven, imprisoning her. The betrayal stung, lancing past her skin searing through to her heart. She'd struggled to keep a certain emotional distance from Chase, just in case, but this latest act scored a burning hole in her trust.

"You can run along, dear. I've got to get ready for a charity lunch."

Laura followed Chase's mother to the door. She managed to exit without tripping over anything through the blur of tears that refused to go anywhere but straight down her cheeks. In her

car, she leaned her head on the steering column
and wept.

"Chase, how could you break my heart again?"

Chapter 12

Laura didn't leave for campus until Sunday morning. She'd managed to get bounced off her flight due to the airline overbooking. Soon after she'd heard the news from Mrs. Westfield and returned home, she'd been ready to jump on a flight to follow Chase. Haley had managed to talk some sense into her. She was too emotional to manage any discussion. Every time her cell phone rang, she expected Chase to be the caller. It never was.

Once she pulled her luggage off the carousel,

she headed for the parking garage. Outside of the bustle of Atlanta's airport area, she dreaded the drive to her apartment. Time hadn't eased her reaction to what Chase had done. Every time she thought about their night at the hotel, their discussions about work and little bits of conversation where they talked about their future together, she started crying. Even Beth had begun calling her the Water Company. She fumbled with the key in the lock, not really seeing through the veil of tears.

"You're home." Omar opened the door to help her with her suitcase. "So did Pierce blow a blood vessel because I went to a friend's for Thanksgiving?" Then he noticed that she was crying. "What happened?" He rushed out the apartment.

Laura had to laugh at his skinny legs running down the steps. "Don't worry, I defended your absence."

"Did someone do something to you?" he yelled up the stairs.

"Omar, come up here. You're making a spectacle. I'll tell you inside." She was sure that some of the nosey neighbors had their ears pinned to the door.

"Is this about Chase?"

She nodded. "Has he called?" She hated to sound like a small child.

"No, but he's in your room. I thought it was strange that he was so quiet."

"In my room?" She bumped Omar out of the way and ran down the hallway. She pushed open the door to find him sitting in the chair staring at the TV.

"What the heck is going on with you?" She didn't know where to begin. He'd left, but didn't tell her. Now, he sat in her room, as if nothing happened. Hearing a noise behind her, she turned around to see Omar standing in the hallway mouthing if she was okay. She nodded. A few minutes later he left the apartment.

"I went to see you on Friday."

Chase turned off the TV. "My mother happily told me what happened, including what she told you."

"So, it's not true?" Laura planned to throttle his mother if she interfered with them again. Thank goodness Haley hadn't let her leave like a crazy woman. She ran over and hugged him. "Why haven't you called?"

Chase pulled her away from him, but held her

hands. She tried to look at him, but he kept his gaze averted. Her unease returned, increasing with each second.

Chase hadn't denied anything.

Laura disengaged herself from him and retreated to the edge of her bed. She took a seat clasping her hands together, waiting. Her heart thudded against her chest. She kept repeating that he couldn't do this to her again.

"I'm waiting, Chase." All warmth had dripped out of her voice.

"A few months ago, my coach wanted to know when I was returning to the field. Truly, I'd thought about it but not in a serious capacity. You were back in my life. I have this job, here. I felt on top of the world."

"Once he put that thought in your head, you started to think about it some more." Laura didn't have to be an athlete to understand the pressure. She'd seen it with Chase and his coach in their better days. And she'd seen it with Chase and Ned.

"Something like that. I don't want an either-or situation. I know that I can have both because I'm older now and can handle the responsibilities."

"When were you going to let me in on this important decision in your life? No phone call. no e-mail. I suppose this is what you consider communicating." She folded her hands to stop her fidgeting. Desperately she wanted to stay in his life, but not at all costs.

He shrugged. "I think that I do want to try for Olympics. I've been working on my drills."

"In secret."

"There's still no guarantees given the injuries, but my coach thinks that's not going to be a problem."

"Well, whatever coach says, right?" She stood up and headed to the kitchen. Her throat was dry from all the crying. Plus she needed to think. Maybe his mother was right. She shouldn't be selfish and hinder him from accomplishing his dream. She heard him approach.

"I love you so much that my head hurts to think of life without you. But loving you isn't enough. Once I'm in training, I'm too focused to be of any good to you. I won't pay you attention. I'll be in a zone. I'm afraid that the training will rip us apart to the point beyond repair."

Laura listened and tried to understand. She

couldn't. She continued drinking her glass of water with her back to him.

"Talk to me," he said.

"You're so focused on the end result that you miss the important things along the way. You continue to shut out the world and when you're ready to reenter, it may be cold and indifferent to you."

Laura set down the glass and turned to him. "In the past six months, where are the millions of fans who clamored for your autograph? Who has stepped up to be the next best racer in your absence? Have the companies kept up their barrage to endorse their products? Have you bothered in the short time that we've reconnected to think beyond yourself? Was I part of the new goal *after* your career petered? Have I been conquered? Should I hail the victorious hero?" She walked toward him and cupped the side of his face. It took every effort not to kiss and lay her cheek against his. This was her man, the owner of her heart and he couldn't understand or accept that gift. "Go your way, Chase. I wish you luck. Now it's time for me to go my way." She dropped her hand and stepped back. She wanted him to grab her and pull her against his chest, saying that he'd made a big mistake. The seconds ticked by and he remained standing with his head lowered. She glanced at his face and saw the deep sadness etched in his features. She leaned over and kissed the side of his mouth. "Don't beat yourself up. I'm okay with your decision." She went to her bedroom and stayed there until she heard the front door close.

Laura stood there for a second. She'd spent enough time crying. Now she felt worn down, tired and exhausted. She needed somebody to pep her up or she'd be bawling like a baby over a man that didn't want her. She called Kasey.

"Hey, Girl, what are you doing tonight?"

"Laura? You're back? I'm not doing too much. Hanging tight, laying low. Work is tomorrow."

"Yeah, I know. Felt like going for a drink. Want to join me?"

"Not tonight. Can I get a raincheck?"

"Get off the phone— " a man's voice interrupted. Kasey giggled. "Got to go, Laura." She hung up the phone before Laura could respond.

"I must be losing my mind," Laura said aloud. "Was that Omar?" she gasped and started laughing hysterically. Wait until he got home and wait until she got to work. Well, at least someone else was having fun.

Laura didn't see much of Chase. She went out of her way not to be in the same room. If that couldn't be helped, she kept as much physical distance between them as possible. He called her a couple of times, but she always let it go to her voicemail, then erased it. He'd even given Omar a note, which she ripped to tiny pieces and flushed it in the toilet.

Omar didn't want to get involved, taking the high road, since she'd teased him unmercifully for dating an older woman. He only put up a weak defense that he wasn't really seeing Kasey. Maybe he should've shared that with Kasey since she preened about having a hot young thing like Omar.

Of course, on general principle, Laura threatened her that, if she hurt her little brother, she'd kick her butt back to Po Dunk, Georgia, where she grew up.

"Have you heard the latest?" Kasey popped her head over the cubicle.

Laura put down the paperwork that needed to be reviewed. "What is it?" Kasey could be so annoying when she had news.

"You're not going to like what I have to say. And don't get all weepy on me. I know that you don't know this and you know I got your back, and all. People think that I run through my men, but I don't let their foolishness get to me. A good man may be hard to find, but you sure can have fun getting there, you know what I mean?" Kasey held up her hand for a high-five.

"Kasey, if you don't start making sense, I'm going to wring your neck." Laura knew somewhere in all that chatter, the news wasn't good.

"Chase announced his resignation. He won't be back in January. I heard the administration isn't too happy. Now there's a press release scheduled for Chase at three this afternoon. Are you coming?"

Laura shook her head. Curiosity grabbed her. She'd rather eat liver and onions than listen to Chase and his coach talk about his future. Anyway, between Kasey and Omar, one of them would tell her everything and whatever else they'd heard in the rumor patch.

In two days, the university closed to begin the holiday schedule. The festive air on campus did little to lighten Laura's mood. First, the data that her department collected basically to determine whether they would still have jobs had been turned in. However, there was no word on the final decision.

Frankly, the rocky road that she seemed to be traveling with Chase didn't excite her to stay with the university if he'd continued working there. The plan to remain unattached and play the scene like a single woman with no desire to be tethered to any man failed. She certainly didn't want to be with any man. She only wanted Chase and all his complexities. Chase had managed to make a spectacular departure. Guess his ego hadn't suffered from the hiatus.

Laura drove home that night without turning on the radio, or her TV when she arrived at her apartment. Instead, she printed off the instructions for the Kwanzaa celebration. She and her niece planned to observe the tradition for the first time in the family after the Christmas holiday was over.

Once she'd completed that task, she grabbed

the suitcase that she'd packed the night before and headed for the car. Her plane reservation was scheduled for the last flight out that night. She looked forward to being home and around family. Her brave front was starting to fall apart at the mention of Chase's name. Her niece had promised that preparing and celebrating Kwanzaa would make her feel better.

Three hours later, she was back in the guest room in Pierce's house. Due to the lateness of the night, everyone agreed to chat the next day. Laura sank into bed, grateful that she was too tired to carry a coherent thought. Omar opted to stay with Sheena when he arrived on Christmas Eve, since he felt that Bobby was being condemned by a bunch of angry women.

The Christmas holidays passed in a whirl of dinners, presents and church service. Pierce looked like the proud patriarch with the entire family present, including Sheena, her husband and their son. Everyone had paused in their bickering, especially Omar and Pierce to celebrate the time of the year. There was always a bit of nostalgia and sadness as they remembered their mother.

Laura was glad to see everyone show up, as she and Beth had requested, on the day after Christmas. She gave a nod to Beth to begin her presentation. Laura tapped her water glass with her knife to cease the discussions around the table. "Beth has something important to say."

Haley looked surprised and almost a little nervous. Laura and Beth hadn't told anyone about their plan for the next seven days.

"Today, December 26, is the first day of the Kwanzaa celebration. This year we're going to celebrate it here. Laura and I are going to lead each day with the principles and then end on January 1 with the meditation."

No one spoke. Laura looked at Pierce to gauge his reaction as a barometer for the rest. She'd like to see everyone participate. But she wouldn't force or sway anyone.

"I'm not sure that it's appropriate since we celebrate Christmas," Haley objected.

"But, Mom, it doesn't replace any religious observances. It's to celebrate our family, community and culture."

"Honey, do you know anything about Kwanzaa?" Haley asked Pierce.

"Only what I see on TV." He turned to Beth. "Why do you want to celebrate this?"

"Because I have a new family, I'm in a new community and I had a little adjusting to do with the culture," she giggled. "But regardless we love each other, right?"

"Of course," Haley piped up.

Everyone murmured their assent. Laura beamed. She was so proud of her niece.

"What do you need us to do?" Pierce inquired. The matter had been settled.

Beth explained, without looking at her notes, "We'll need to create a space in the family room for the Kwanzaa set where the table with the African symbols will be. There'll be the *kinara* which holds the seven candles in red, black and green. We must think about our people, the struggle and the future."

Laura pulled out the candles for them to see. She held up three red ones and three green ones. Beth held up the only black candle. "This represents unity," she said in a clear voice. "On the left of the black candle will be the red candles for self-determination, cooperative economics and crea tivity." Beth took a steadying breath.

Laura touched her shoulder, reassuring her that she was doing a good job. She could see the pleasant surprise on Haley's face as she watched her daughter.

"The three green candles on the left represent collective work and responsibility, purpose and faith. At the table will be corn, books and a unity cup for libation to the ancestors. Come with me to light the first candle."

Everyone followed Beth with solemn expressions. Her serious toned delivery set a contemplative mood. The table had already been set with the hope that Pierce would agree. They formed a semicircle, waiting for Beth to proceed.

"Today's principle is *Umoja,* which means Unity. We will light the black candle after we go through the greeting."

"And that means what?" Pierce still looked skeptical.

"Striving for unity within the community, our race, and family and nation," Beth explained. "Each evening, we'll begin with a principle. For instance, tonight's principle is Unity. There is a general greeting where I'll always say—*Habari Gani?* And all of you would say *Umoja.* Every day you'd answer with the next principle: *Kujichagulia, Ujima, Ujamaa, Nia, Kuumba, Imani.*"

Laura saw Pierce frown. "We'll provide the words and their meanings on paper each day." The news erased his frown.

"Isn't there a party or something on the last day?" Haley questioned.

"The first day of the year is Kwanzaa's last day. It's very important that we do think about where we are today and where we need to be tomorrow, we need to think about our present, as well as the past. We are to rededicate our commitment to our highest ideals. We can use it as a day of remembrance, assessment and meditation. I have invited several people to celebrate with us. The list is confidential."

This last piece of news surprised Laura. Beth had a little sneakiness in her. Didn't matter, she probably invited her entire class. It'd be good to see who some of her friends turned out to be.

New Year's day was simply the first day of the year. The day didn't hold any special meaning, until they had chosen to celebrate Kwanzaa. Beth was over the top with her excitement to begin the last day of the ceremony. The family had gathered in the family room. No one else had arrived. Laura hoped that her niece wouldn't be too disappointed that her invitees didn't show.

When the door bell sounded, she hurriedly answered, breathing a sigh of relief. Chase was the last person she expected to see standing at her doorstep. She looked over her shoulder, making sure no one realized who was there.

"I've been hoping to catch you alone."

Laura stared, mainly because she still couldn't believe that he was on her porch.

"I've missed you."

Laura didn't respond. He knew before they went their separate ways that she would miss him and would always love him, but that didn't mean that they were right for each other. She had been slow to learn that fact, but now it was very clear.

"I start training in a week."

"I've got to be heading back." Back to her retreat in the guest room until she returned to work in Atlanta.

"Looks like we may be seeing...I mean running into each other on campus."

"Why?" He did say that he was going to be training.

"I'm training on campus. It was my compromise for leaving the university."

"Lucky them," she said, with added sarcasm. Well, at the least the university got some type of concession. What did she get?

"I also thought it would be a way to stay closer to you."

"What about the zone? You know, your one person solitary confinement."

"I haven't been the best communicator. There were things that I didn't think you could understand. I wanted this part of my life over because I didn't like who I became. When I didn't win and got injured, I felt lost and angry. I couldn't possibly put you through that emotional rollercoaster. But I can't live without you either. There's one thing that I told my coach that I need your response to."

"Response to what?"

"I said that I'd go back to the track, but only if you accepted my marriage proposal."

The blood rushed to Laura's head, making her dizzy with emotional intoxication.

"Laura, will you marry me?"

"You're making my head spin," Laura groaned, rubbing her temples.

"Ever since we reconnected, I told you that I loved you."

Luara nodded. "And how many times did you waffle?" As she uttered the words, her reasoning came back into focus. Thank goodness. The silly giddiness that she desperately tried to tamp down had no place in this discussion.

"I asked Pierce for your hand."

"How medieval of you." Wow! She wanted to throw up her hands in celebration. "Well, what did he say?" Laura raised her chin, ready to do battle with either answer, just for the heck of it.

"Actually, he said that I should give you your space. When you're ready to deal with a 'bozo' like me, you will do so on your own time."

Laura couldn't help the chuckle that escaped. Chase looked quite uncomfortable. "What about your mother?"

"The idea is growing on her. Let's not worry about our family members, mine especially." He winked. "Let's go back inside."

They reentered the house. Laura stopped in midstride looking at the balloons and streamers decorating the hallway that had been bare minutes earlier. She turned to Chase, who shrugged.

"Surprise! Congratulations!" Her family jumped out from their hiding places.

Laura shrieked and stepped back, bumping into Chase.

"Not yet." He waved them into silence.

"What's going on?"

"We have a surprise engagement party," Haley explained.

"Oh, do you now?" Laura looked at the faces grinning back at her and then at Chase who looked miserable. She finally got what this was all about and she was momentarily speechless. "We're not engaged."

"What!" The collective question poked at her with their outrage.

"Chase, since you got this little party to celebrate another one of your accomplishments, I'd like to hear why you think that I should give you the time of day."

"Ooh," Beth giggled and Haley clamped a restraining hand over her daughter's mouth.

"I love you."

"Heard that before."

"I'm committed to being your loving husband."

Laura rolled her eyes. No need to tell him that her resolve disintegrated with every declaration.

"You keep me grounded. You're my rock, my salvation, my inspiration."

"Oh, enough already." Chase's father stepped into the group. A loud cheer erupted.

Laura felt someone touch her arm. She turned and was standing six inches away from Mrs. Westfield. Although she was surrounded by her family, the woman's presence rattled her.

"Laura, Chase and I have had a long discussion about how deeply he cares for you and how much he wants you in his life. I know that you may judge my words as insincere. But, I'm not. Since you make my son incredibly happy, I am happy and thankful for you in his life."

The group quieted for an intense moment before clapping. Laura actually saw perspiration pepper his mother's brow. They didn't embrace, but at least they'd moved in a positive direction. She accepted his token of friendship.

"Since I missed the question the first time, let me hear you ask one more time?" Laura waved away the groans.

Chase dropped to one knee and held out his hand with the charm bracelet and a large canary solitaire in his palm. It was the same gift he'd presented to her the day she'd arrived on the job. "Laura Masterson, will you marry me, please?"

Laura had been waiting since childhood to answer the question.

"Yes."

A brand-new story of love
and drama from...

national bestselling author
MARCIA
KING-GAMBLE

All
ABOUT
ME

Big-boned beauty Chere Adams
plunges into an extreme makeover
to capture the eye of fitness fanatic
Quentin Abraham—but the more
she changes, the less he seems to
notice her. Is it possible Quentin's
more interested in the old Chere?

*Available the first week of January
wherever books are sold.*

KIMANI
ROMANCE

www.kimanipress.com   KPMKG0010107

Winning her love wouldn't be so easy
the second time around...

HERE
and
NOW

Favorite author
Michelle Monkou

When Chase Dillard left Laura Masterson years ago to pursue
his Olympic dreams, he broke her heart. Now that they're
working together, Chase has lots of ground to make up if he
wants to win her back.

KIMANI™
ROMANCE

www.kimanipress.com

KPMM0020107